Another Shot

By:

Brooke St. James

ii

Chapter 1

It's extremely dramatic and maybe even a bit overdone to begin the story at a funeral, but I'm doing it anyway. That's just the way it's got to be since it was a major turning point in my life. Four days ago, everything changed in an instant, and now, at this very moment, I found myself staring at an arrangement of flowers that hung over my husband's closed coffin.

You heard me right.

I had the wrong idea about widows. In my mind, that word applied to old, or at least *older* women. Twenty-three certainly didn't feel like the right age to obtain that title, but there I was, staring at a big, wooden box that contained...

I put my face in my hands, and tears freely fell. It was no use trying to contain them. My mother-in-law was sitting next to me and she felt me take a breath in between sobs, which started her crying again as well. I could feel her begin to shake, and it made me cry even harder.

The car accident that took my husband, also took his father and brother, which meant Laura Milano lost her husband and two sons in one fell swoop.

I was married to her younger son Anthony, and her older son, Tommy, was married to a girl named

Anna. Anna was sitting on the other side of Laura, and the three of us were huddled on the front pew, waiting for someone to speak. My late father-in-law, Gianni, had a business partner named Vinny, and I was relatively sure he would be doing the honors, but I couldn't be certain. I didn't really care who was speaking, as long as it wasn't me.

I felt a wave of anxiety hit me, causing cold sweats and nausea flood my body. For a few seconds I thought I might pass out. I wanted to leave as quickly as my feet would take me, but I stayed for Laura's sake.

She sobbed loudly with no regard for the rows and rows of people sitting in the church pews behind us. It had been four days since the accident, and you'd think we'd be all cried out, but tears continued to stream. My face ached and my eyes burned, and more than once I thanked God that Laura made me wear a black veil.

I glanced up to see that someone was making his way to the microphone. I begged myself to become distracted so I could avoid wailing uncontrollably. I stared at him. *That's Vinny. Look at him. Look at his suit. It's a grey suit. You should look at his grey suit.* I stared at the faint plaid pattern, trying to do anything but remember why we were there.

"I remember when Gianni first came to me and said, 'we should move to Arizona,'" Vinny said, testing the mic with that first statement. He settled on a place to hold it and regarded the crowd. "It was

4

twenty years ago. The boys were babies." He paused, clinched his eyes shut, and put a fist to his mouth at the thought of the boys. Laura cried uncontrollably, and I sobbed right along with her. We held onto each other tightly in an effort to keep it together so Vinny could finish his speech.

We must have been doing a pretty good job, because Vinny was talking again. I wasn't sure how much of his speech I missed while I was trying to get myself together; I was so out of it that it was hard to tell. It was impossible to focus on anything— impossible to form a coherent chain of thoughts.

Anthony and his family were all I had, so like Laura, *everything* had been taken away from me in that accident. My thoughts during Vinny's speech were desperate and delirious, and jumped around to random things. I barely heard what he was saying. Every time I tuned in, I'd hear something that made me start crying, so mostly I just didn't listen.

Tommy's wife, Anna, was one of four girls, and she had her whole family there to support her. Her mom was sitting right next to her, and her sisters were also on the front row, down a little ways. I, on the other hand, had no family, so I physically clung to Laura as we did our best to get through the funeral.

Swimming.

My head was swimming. My thoughts were swimming. There was a wet, swimmy quality to the whole day that I thought might be a result of all the tears. There were a lot of people at the funeral. A lot of people I didn't even recognize. I spoke to a few of them, but all of my interactions felt as if I was floating in a fishbowl and the people I was talking to were outside breathing real air. I normally communicated with people just fine, but today was different; my encounters were warped and surreal.

By the time we went back to Laura's house, my face and head throbbed painfully. The service and burial were over, but Laura had a house full of people who stayed until past dinner time. By 9PM there were only four of us left.

Anthony and I shared a rent house with Tommy and Anna while we each saved for down payments to put toward our own place. Neither Anna nor I had spent the night at the house since we lost the boys. I was staying at Laura's and she at her parents' house.

Anna and her mother had just gone home, which left me, Vinny, Laura, and her brother Joey who'd flown in from New Jersey.

I was lying on the couch with my eyes closed— had been for quite some time. Anna and her family assumed I was sleeping and were careful not to wake me on their way out. My head was throbbing so badly that I didn't bother to explain that I was awake.

"We need to talk," I heard Joey say right when the door closed. I knew it was Joey who spoke because his East Coast accent was a lot heavier than Vinny's. "I know it's not a good time, Laura, but we really need to talk about the logistics of everything."

"What's that supposed to mean?" I heard her ask.

"I've been talking to Vinny. You need to know that there's some things Gianni wasn't honest with you about." There were a few seconds of silence. "About the business," he continued.

"I really hope you don't have bad news for me, Joey, because right now I don't know if I can—"

"It's pretty bad," Vinny said. "I'm sorry, Laura. We've barely been keeping our heads above water. It's been like this since Bellman expanded."

Gianni and Vinny were partners in a car dealership that specialized in high-end used cars, but five years ago when Rob Bellman of Bellman Toyota, Bellman Nissan, and Bellman Subaru expanded his dealership to include a mega used car lot, their business started going downhill.

Anthony and Tommy must have known the state of affairs, because I'd heard them discussing other business ventures when their dad wasn't around.

"We owe a scary amount of money to the IRS, and we haven't been able to make payments to Frankie, but we have quite a bit tied up in cars right now, and I think if we sell everything, we'll be able to pay at least *some* of what we owe."

"We can't sell the business," Laura said, sounding shocked. "That's how we make a living. It's all we have."

"You can't have that business," Joey said.

He sounded heartless, and I ached for Laura. I considered going to her for support, but my head weighed a thousand pounds. Plus, I knew they'd never be having this conversation if they thought I was awake.

"Keeping the business isn't an option," Vinny said, with at least some regret in his tone. "I'm sorry that it had to come at a time like this, but we need to unload it."

"Why do we still owe Frankie money?" Laura asked. "I thought we paid him back years ago."

"We did pay him back… for what he gave us to start the business, but we borrowed some more a few years ago when we got all those cars from the auction."

"Gianni didn't tell me you borrowed money from him again," she said.

Several seconds of silence passed.

"I don't know what to tell you," Vinny said. "I guess he didn't want you to worry."

Laura huffed a laugh, then more silence, followed by, "How much?"

"We borrowed a hundred, but we've paid twenty or thirty, I think."

"A hundred *thousand*?" she asked in disbelief.

"Seventy or eighty now."

"How much do we owe the IRS?"

Vinny and Joey both made sounds that let her know it was bad news. "A lot," Vinny said. "We kept thinking it would get better, but we spent the last few years robbing Peter to pay Paul."

"How much do we have tied up in the business?" she asked.

"We ran the numbers. We think we'll be able to pay the IRS in full and only owe Frankie sixty. I figured we'd just split the responsibility since that's how it's always been. That means you'll owe him about thirty." He paused, but then continued. "These numbers are just an estimate."

"So, not only do I have no business, but now you're telling me I'm *indebted* to someone with nothing to show for it?"

"I'm sorry, Laura, but there's really no other time to talk about this," Vinny said. "We need to start wrapping things up right away."

"I can't *owe* someone thirty thousand dollars," Laura said, using the same, stunned tone of voice. "I can't even pay the mortgage if the business doesn't exist, let alone pay Frankie back for money I didn't even know we borrowed."

"That's exactly why we need to have this conversation, Laura," Joey said. "I'm leaving tomorrow, but I wanted to help you get started listing the house and making arrangements to come back home."

A whole minute of silence followed by a screeching chair and then Laura saying, "Don't touch me," with a sob.

I literally couldn't move, and even if I could, I knew there was nothing I could do to help her. I barely cracked my eyes open, and could see their

9

outlines from across two rooms. It looked like Joey was standing next to Laura and Vinny was a few feet from them. I closed my eyes again because they were too heavy to keep open.

"I have a life here, Joey. I am not moving back to New York."

"You can't pay for this life, Laura."

"I already talked to Frankie," Vinny said. "You know he's into real estate. He said he's got an apartment in the city that's vacant right now."

"I never said I was moving!" she said angrily. "Are *you* moving back?" she asked Vinny.

"No, but Linda and I have the day care business, and we're—"

"What makes you think you can make plans for me to move across the country without even consulting me?" Her tone was extremely angry and sounded like she was on the verge of bursting into tears.

"You don't really have a choice," Vinny said sadly. "You owe on your house and your car, and there's just no way to keep them."

Another minute of silence passed. I heard movement, but I didn't peek.

"I can't believe he left me with *nothing*," she said. "Less than nothing!" She sighed. "So I'm supposed to sell everything I own and move to New York where I'll be living in one of Frankie's apartments?"

"Yes."

"The same Frankie that I also mysteriously owe thirty thousand dollars?"

"There's nothing mysterious about it," Joey said. "Gianni borrowed that money, and Vinny's only responsible for half."

"It might not be thirty," Vinny said, "That's just an estimate."

"Frankie's doing you a favor, Laura," Joey said. "His place isn't far from the apartment. He said you can clean it in exchange for rent."

"Like an indentured servant," she said, frustrated.

"You don't have any other choice," Joey said. "Maggie and I can't do anything to help, or we would. We do our best to get by. We have one thinking about college and the other in braces. Frankie's our best option here. He loved Gianni and the boys. He's doing you a favor with this offer."

I heard her crying, and my body just shut down as a way of dealing with the bitter sadness that now gripped me. I drifted in and out of delirious sleep for a while. I heard her yelling in an angry tone that God had forsaken her, and I stirred and vaguely wondered if I was dreaming. I peeked into the kitchen to see that Joey was holding Laura, who was crying.

The next time I woke up the room was empty. I was covered by a blanket that hadn't been there before I fell asleep, but I didn't remember anyone giving it to me. My eyes still burned and ached from

11

shedding so many tears, and I figured it hadn't been that long since I fell asleep. I peered at the little clock on the cable box, but it was blurry and I quickly gave up trying to see it.

I didn't care what time it was. It was the saddest day of my life, and it couldn't be over fast enough. I stayed there with my eyes closed, wishing I'd wake up to find out that this was all a big nightmare. I was relatively sure that before I went to sleep I heard Laura say she had to move away. I wasn't ready to give her up. Losing Anthony was a crippling blow that was only softened by the fact that I had Laura.

My mom wasn't ready to have children when she got pregnant with me. She left me with her parents, who were functioning alcoholics. They provided a decent enough place for me to live, but my grandma died a few years ago, and my grandpa's gone downhill since then. The VA put him in an assisted living facility and he recognizes me less and less each time I go in.

I'd never heard from my mom. My grandma told me a little about her, saying she thought she lived in Detroit. I knew her name and could probably try to get in touch, but I never had. All this to say, Anthony and his beautiful family were basically all I had, and now they were gone.

Chapter 2

"I'm going with you." I moaned.

I thought the words would come out properly, but the grief rested on me like a heavy cloud, causing everything to be slurred and blurred. It came out more like a moan.

"Hey sleepyhead," Laura said. She was sitting at the table in her robe—her hand around the coffee mug that rested on the table. I stared at her as I shuffled into the kitchen. She tried to smile when she called me sleepyhead, but the gesture couldn't break through the mask of sadness.

Anna was sitting at the table across from her with her back to me. She turned with a slightly more convincing smile to greet me as I approached. I glanced at the clock, which read 10:32.

"I slept late," I said. Again, my voice was giving me trouble, but I got it out and they seemed to understand me.

"I tried not to wake you when I came in," Anna said.

"I didn't hear anything," I said as I sleepily settled into the chair next to her. They had both showered and changed since the funeral, and I was still wearing remnants of my black mourning clothes. I was extremely out of it, and wondered if they were too.

"Coffee helps a little bit," Laura said, reading my mind. "Do you want me to make you a cup?"

"I'll get up and get it in a second," I said. I stacked my arms on the table and used them as a pillow, resting my head and closing my eyes.

"I called Anna over here this morning to talk about some things," Laura said. "I wanted to wait till you woke up to fill you girls in on some things Joey and Vinny told me last night."

It was then that I remembered what I'd been trying to say right when I woke up. "I'm going with you," I said, lifting my head and regarding Laura from across the table.

She and Anna both looked at me with perplexed expressions.

"I heard your conversation," I explained.

Laura searched my face. "What did you hear?"

"That you have to move to New York."

Anna gasped and put a hand over her mouth and Laura looked at her with a regretful expression.

"Is it true?" Anna asked.

"I'm afraid it is. My brother's there, and Gianni's cousin Frankie who's helped us out in the past. I've got to sell the house and car lot, so staying here isn't really an option."

"You can't leave," Anna said.

I glanced at her to see tears well in her eyes. I knew exactly how she felt. Laura's eyes filled with tears at the sight of Anna's.

"I can't even begin to tell you how sad this makes me," Laura said. She spoke in a slow, even tone and put a hand to her chest. "You girls are my heart, and to have to leave you right after this happened... " She blinked and tears fell onto her cheeks. "I just keep thinking it can't get any worse. I feel like God has completely forsaken me."

"I'm going with you," I said.

"Me too," Anna said. "Or we'll figure out a way for us all to stay."

Laura shook her head.

"I heard the whole conversation last night when I was half-asleep. I knew before I even walked in here this morning that I was going. I was trying to say it when I walked in. I'm going with you, Laura. I've already thought about it. I can help you."

"I'll go too," Anna said.

Laura's pain showed on her face as she stared at us, deciding what to say. "You have no idea how much it touches my heart that you would even say something like this." Silent tears streamed down her face as she continued. "But the truth is, I have nothing to offer you. It kills me to admit this, but I truly believe God has turned his back on me. If you came with me, I'd just bring you down."

"I've already thought about it," I said. "I'm going."

Laura put a hand in the air. "Just hear me out. Believe me, it pains me to think about leaving you girls. I love you so much, and..." she paused, and wiped her eyes with the sleeve of her robe. "…I have no one over there. I haven't been back in twenty years. I'm a stranger to them. I'm just an old woman with no connections or sons for you to marry." She blinked and tears rolled onto her cheeks. "Stay here and find yourselves good men. You'll have good lives, and raise a family. You would have a much easier time doing that here. I have no prospects for you in New York." Laura reached over the corner of the table, and Anna and I put our hands in hers. We sort of all huddled in an awkward hug.

"I can't believe you have to go," Anna said, beginning to sob. "I'm gonna miss you so much."

We cried together, much the same as we'd been doing for the last four days. We were all holding onto each other, and I gave Laura a squeeze. "I'm seriously going," I said.

She wiped at her eyes. "You can't," she said. "I can't do that to you. I have nothing to give you. I have debts, and—"

"I can help you. I want to help you." I shook her arms and looked into her bloodshot eyes.

"Anna's doing the right thing," Laura said, begging me with her expression to stop making it so difficult. "She's staying here with her mom, and it's the right choice." She squeezed my arm. "I know you love me, Rae. There's not a doubt in my mind that you do. I love you too."

Anna continued to wipe at her eyes as I stared at Laura.

"Please don't ask me to leave you again," I said, crying. "Wherever you go, I want to go. I want to live where you live. I want to be a part of what family you have over there, and if that turns out to be nobody, then I'll just be with you." I squeezed her again. "Please understand how important it is for me to stay with you. I'm not letting you go alone."

I could tell by the way Laura stared at me that she finally understood I was serious.

"I don't know when you have to leave, but I can take care of things here," Anna said, practically.

"Vinny's taking care of the car lot. He's helping with the car and house too."

"When were you thinking about leaving?" Anna asked.

"Thursday. I've been on the phone all morning. Joey helped me rent a truck. Vinny's gonna help me get my things into it and when I get to New York, Frankie will help me unload."

"When *we* get to New York," I said.

She let a hint of a smile touch her lips. "When we get to New York," she said softly.

I smiled even though it hurt my face. I knew it was the right decision. Every bone in my body was telling me to go with her.

***

It had been exactly a week since the accident, and the whole situation still seemed surreal. I wondered if I'd ever feel normal again, or if the shock of everything had somehow permanently altered me. It was Thursday when Laura and I took off, headed for New York in the mid-size U-Haul truck her brother, Joey, reserved. We resolved to take turns driving, but I took the first shift.

Anthony and I each had a car. I knew I couldn't sell them for what we owed on them in such short notice, but Vinny worked it out where the dealership bought them back before we left.

I had about ten boxes of personal belongings and just over a thousand dollars to my name. Anthony kept track of all the money, so I had no idea what we had until I went to the bank to withdraw it. He and I had been saving for a down payment on a house for the year we'd been married, and I was surprised to find that there was only a thousand dollars. I was convinced that I was making the right choice, though, and had to trust that everything would be okay.

I felt a little better about my financial prospects after Laura spoke with Frankie on the phone during that first day driving. It was on speakerphone so I could hear the whole conversation.

"Hey Frankie."

"Hey Lulu, where you at?"

"Don't call me that."

"Why not? I called you that since I can remember."

"That's a happy name, Frankie, and I'm not a happy woman."

He was silent, for a second, and when he continued, he sounded considerably less cheerful. "When are you ladies planning on rollin' into town?"

"Saturday night if all goes as planned. Joey said we can sleep in Jersey if we don't want to mess with traffic in the city, in which case it'll be Sunday."

"Let me know what you decide, and I'll send some boys to unload your things. I went by the apartment today. It's in good shape, but you should know that the second room is barely fit to be an office. I list it as a one bedroom. You could probably fit a single bed in there but not much else. I hope the girl isn't claustrophobic."

I glanced at Laura from across the truck and she gave me a regretful smile. I smiled back letting her know I'd be just fine with whatever accommodations were awaiting.

"The good news is, I think I got her a job lined up."

"How'd you do that?" she asked.

"You remember Big Willie Russo. His oldest boy has that camera place down on 53rd. It's right down the street from the apartment. Anyway, he does a lot of online business, and he's always looking for people in the shipping department."

"Have you already talked to him?" she asked.

"Yep," he said proudly. "I ran into him at the deli earlier and told him you were coming back to town and bringing your daughter-in-law. He said he'd email with instructions. She'll probably just be able

19

to say Dominic sent her and they'll hand her a nametag. It won't be much, but it'll get her started and she can work her way up."

I glanced at Laura again, and we shared a little smile.

"We're gonna pay you back, Frankie," Laura said. "Rae's gonna help me, and we're gonna make good on what the boys borrowed."

"Just get here," he said. "It'll be fine." I could tell by his tone that he didn't believe in a million years that Laura would be able to keep that promise. If anything, he probably expected to spend money on us rather than get paid back. Well, we would just have to prove him wrong.

They said their goodbyes and she hung up with him a minute later. "It's good that Willie's boy wants to give you a job," was the first thing she said when she hung up the phone. "The Russo's are a good family. I knew about Dominic's camera business. I think it'll be a good place to start, like Frankie said."

Laura and I drove for three days straight. It was late Saturday when we got close, so we decided to stop in New Jersey for the night. Joey and his wife, Maggie, were kind hosts and made us feel welcome, but it was late when we got there, and we really didn't talk much before going to bed.

They only had one spare bedroom, so Laura and I shared the queen size bed. September was much cooler in New Jersey than it was in Arizona, and I slept like a rock under the thick comforter.

We got an early start the next morning. We ate a quick breakfast before getting in the truck to follow Joey and Maggie into the city.

There were two Italians in leather coats standing outside when we parked on the street in front of the apartment building.

"Lulu Milano, you look like a million bucks!" The bigger one yelled when we got out of the truck.

"Don't call her Lulu," the other one said.

The bigger one looked at him with a sarcastic smile. "Yeah, and I suppose you don't wanna be called Frankie either," he said nudging the smaller guy, who I now knew was Frankie.

"He's right. I don't wanna be called Lulu," Laura said. She offered a sad smile and reached out to give a sideways hug to the guy who'd said it. "It's a happy name, and that's a word that no longer applies to me."

"I'm sorry," the big one said.

"It's okay." She sighed and put a hand on my shoulder as I came to stand beside her. "I've got Rae to help me through."

Frankie came over and took us both into his arms at the same time, giving us a tight squeeze. My cheek pressed into the cold leather on his lapel. "You girls are gonna get through this," he said with conviction. "I'm sorry for your loss. We loved Gianni and the boys."

My eyes burned and I did my best to hold back the tears that threatened to come out at the mention

21

of Anthony. I distracted myself by staring at the big guy's haircut. I stared at it thinking about how much product he must have to use to make it slick back like that. I never saw men in Arizona wear their hair like that, and I enjoyed the distraction of imagining him combing it in the mirror like the movie Grease.

Frankie greeted Joey and Maggie, who had just gotten out of their car as he released us from the hug. Then he turned to the big guy. "What time are the other two getting here?" he asked.

The guy shrugged and Frankie scowled as he stared down the street to see if they were coming. "I'm Rae," I said extending a hand toward the big guy. Frankie and Laura both apologized at the same time for not introducing us.

"This is Little Mike," Frankie said, slapping Mike's shoulder. Mike shook my hand with a shy smile, and just as we finished our greeting, an old, brown, classic car in restored condition pulled up and two guys who were also very Italian, got out. They spoke to the driver for a second before he drove off, and then they turned to head toward us. Both of them were smiling.

I knew Anthony's family was Italian, but for some reason, it really didn't come across when they were in Arizona. Being here, seeing all these big, dark Italian guys with New York accents, leather coats, and pomade was not at all what I expected. I felt like I was in a scene from Goodfellas. I should have known to expect this with names like Vinny and Frankie, but the level of Italian-ness still came as a surprise.

Chapter 3

"Who ya got with you, Ms. Lu?"

"She ain't Lulu," Little Mike said.

"What took you boys so long?" Frankie said, changing the subject. They ignored him for a second, stopping in front of Laura to look her over. They both stood in front of her with sweet smiles like they didn't know what to say.

"I can't believe you boys are so big," she said. She pointed at the younger one. "You were just a baby the last time I saw you. You probably don't even remember me." She looked at the older one, giving him a sad smile. "You used to play with Tony and Tommy all the time," she said. "I'm sure you remember."

He nodded and smiled. "It's good to see you. Mom cried when she found out you was movin' back home. She's real excited to see you. Dad wouldn't even let us tell her we was movin' you in, or she would be here right now."

Laura smiled. "Tell your mama I'm happy to see her. I'm happy to see you boys too. You went and became men while I was gone."

They both smiled, and she glanced at me. "This here's Rae. She belonged to my Tony and she's what's got me through all this."

She took a deep breath and I knew she was trying not to cry. I stuck my hand out toward the one closest to me.

"I'm Rae."

"Ben."

I shook his hand.

"William," the other one said, when I turned my attention to him.

They were both young, strapping men and all I could think was thank goodness we had help getting these boxes upstairs.

"There's a freight elevator down the hallway on the right," Frankie said, reading my mind. "We can all catch up over dinner sometime, but we should get movin'."

Ben and William both clapped at the same time, looking like a team getting ready to take the field. Thanks to this kind of enthusiasm (and Little Mike's brute strength) we had the truck emptied in no time. Laura stayed in the apartment the whole time, looking through it, imagining where we'd put our things. Maggie mostly stayed out of the way too. I made a few trips to the truck, but the guys kept saying for me to take it easy, so I finally listened and let them finish the job.

Frankie stayed in the apartment with Laura and me while the others got the remaining boxes. Frankie was the oldest in the bunch, and seemed to be in charge. Laura had never mentioned anything about them being mobsters or anything, and maybe it was racist of me to assume something like that just because they were Italian, but Frankie was the epitome of a mob boss—complete with snakeskin boots and gaudy gold jewelry. I liked him—liked the whole scene. I thoroughly enjoyed watching him interact with the other guys, and caught myself feeling thankful for the new beginning.

The place was furnished. It wasn't glamorous, but it was better than anything we could do for ourselves at this point. We sat at the small, vintage table in the dining area that connected to the kitchen.

"There's a few dishes in the cabinet. Pots and pans too. I had some food brought up since I thought you might not feel like shopping. There's a deli with groceries down the block. You'll remember it. We all hang out there still. I was thinking you could do about ten hours a week cleaning for the rent. Does that sound fair?"

"It's more than fair, Frankie, and you know it," Laura said with her head down. The others were out of the room at the moment, and she continued speaking, but stared down at the table, looking ashamed. "I'm sorry you're stuck helping me out again."

He reached over and put a hand on hers. "I'm glad to do it, Laura. Vivian is too. She's real excited you're back."

"I'm not the same person I used to be, Frankie. I'm never gonna be the person you guys remember."

"Sure you are," he said with a little smile. "You're still the same to me."

She smiled but it didn't reach her eyes. "The ten hours a week is more than fair for the place. I'll pick up more work, and with Rae at the camera store, we'll be just fine. We'll work out a payment plan for you as soon as we get on our feet."

"I know you will," said Frankie, "and I'm really not worried about it. We haven't even taken care of the dealership and the house yet. Just get settled and we'll figure it all out." He patted her hand. "If you need anything, we're right down the street."

"It means a lot, Frankie."

"This one's marked for you, Rae. Where's your stuff going?" Ben asked.

"In the nook." I said. I stood so I could offer to help, but they wouldn't let me.

The guys were only there for a little while longer. I had a window in my nook that overlooked the street, and I watched as Joey took off in the truck with Maggie behind him in their car. The brown car pulled up again and William and Ben got inside. Frankie and Little Mike took off on foot down the sidewalk in what I assumed was the direction of Frankie's place.

I had given my email address to Frankie earlier, and I got a message from him that night. It included instructions for showing up to my first day at work at the camera store.

Dominic's assistant sent the message. She said I should go by the store from 2-4 on Thursday and ask to speak to Debbie in shipping and receiving. Debbie would help me work out a schedule and give me all the details for my new job. I liked my old job at the coffee shop, and I caught myself dreading the sound of *shipping and receiving*, but I had faith that I could work up to something better.

***

By the time I'd been on the job for three days, I'd already learned everything there is to know about opening a box with a cutter. Nic's Photo and Video was a much larger business than I expected. I assumed I'd get to know the guy Dominic who'd given me the job, but I was relatively sure he didn't even know I was there. The shipping and receiving area of the store was huge, but it was in the basement, and the receiving section, where I'd been put to work, was a much smaller secluded area near the back of the building.

I worked with three other people every shift, which was nothing compared to the twenty or so that worked in shipping at any given time. It was my job to deal with returned items. I had a little area where I inspected the item and made notes about its condition. It almost always had to be cleared by a tech who'd make sure it was fit to be resold, but I was the first step of the process.

Don't get the wrong idea about it being in the basement. It was, technically, but we had high ceilings with a row of windows at the top, and actually got a good bit of natural light down there. The receiving crew shared a common area, but each of us had our own little cubical as well. We were encouraged to decorate our space however we liked. It was the opposite of a sterile, office environment, which made the job better than I expected. Plus, I got along with my co-workers. Considering that I was dreading being locked away in a shipping and receiving dungeon somewhere, the job wasn't that bad.

Everyone I talked to seemed to love Dominic. They said he was an outstanding boss and that's why his business had taken off the way it had. His store was one of the biggest suppliers of photo and video equipment in the world. Apparently, if I had ordered a nice camera off the internet, (which I hadn't) I would have most likely gotten it from Nic's. Debbie told me that the first day I came when she couldn't believe I'd never heard of it.

I was standing on the far side of the loading bay during my lunch break when a man walked by. He was tall with dark hair wearing jeans and a button-up shirt layered under a jacket. His clothes were stylish and I caught myself straightening just to avoid looking like a total slob next to him.

"Smoke break?" he asked coming to stand next to me.

"Lunch break."

"Did you know there's a park just up the street?"

"Yeah, but I don't mind it back here. It's usually quiet except for the ones who come out to smoke, and they stay over there by the door."

"How long have you been working here?" he asked.

I thought he might be a rep for one of the brands we sold. I could totally see him being a guy who travels around the city selling a product that everyone wants like Canon or Nikon.

"I just started," I said. "I'm working back here in receiving."

"Do you like it?"

I smiled and shrugged. "It's fine," I said. "I worried that I'd hate it, and I definitely don't."

"Would you rather work in another department?" he asked.

I shook my head. "No, I'm fine where I'm at right now. I don't have enough experience to work on the floor anyway. The only photography experience I have is using my camera phone," I said, laughing. "But I'm interested now that I have this job. I think I could get into it now that I'm here checking out all this cool gear. I sort of regret that it's taken me this long to take interest."

He smiled. "It's an amazing art form. You can tell stories with photographs. Do you have any good ones on your phone?" he asked.

The question surprised me, and my thoughts went to the camera roll on my phone. There were a ton of pictures of Anthony on there. The phone was in my bag, but I never even looked at it any more. I didn't see any point since I had the service turned off after Anthony's death.

"I'm in between phones right now, actually," I said shyly.

"What are you doing for pictures?"

"I guess I haven't taken many lately."

"That's a shame." He'd been standing, but now he sat next to me on the curb.

"You need a bench out here," he said.

"It's fine," I said, scooting over to make room for him. "Like you said, there's a park down the street."

"Do you think you'll keep working here?"

"It's hard to tell. I'm thankful for the job, but I had more responsibility at my old one. I'm not saying I don't like this one, but I'm gonna be doing my best to move up or move on pretty quickly."

"What do you think about the boss?"

"His name's Dominic."

"You haven't met him?"

"No. But I've heard he's a good guy. Everyone in there seems to really like him."

Just then, the door opened and a guy I worked with named Matt peered out. "There you are Mr. Russo," he said. "Your assistant said she needs you to call her back as soon as you can."

I looked at Mr. Russo who gave Matt an easy smile.

"I'll text her Matt, thanks for letting me know. And call me Dominic."

Matt smiled and gave a little bow as he closed the door.

I looked over at the guy sitting next to me. "Isn't Dominic Russo the guy who owns this place?"

"Yes."

"And did you just ask me what I thought about him when I didn't know he was you?"

He scrunched up his face as if he was deciphering the question but then smiled and nodded. "Yes."

"You gave me this job."

"That's what I hear," he said. "I was talking to Matt and Debbie earlier. They told me you were the one who came to town with Lulu."

I cringed inwardly at the name Lulu, not wanting her to have to correct him if he called her that. I was so taken aback by this stranger turning out to be Dominic, that I didn't' say anything about.

"Debbie and Matt both said what a great job you're doing."

"They're both really nice," I said. "Everyone is. It's a great place to work. I hope I didn't come across as ungrateful when I said I'd be moving on."

"Not at all," he said. "Receiving's not for everyone."

I smiled at him. "It's great, and I don't take it for granted that the job fell into my lap."

"From what Debbie and Matt tell me we are the lucky ones."

"I don't know if I'd go that far, but I am pretty handy with a box cutter." I drew it out of my back pocket and flashed it. "Fastest hands in the west."

He laughed a deep, rumbling laugh that had me smiling. "I'm pretty sure you should stay at my store," he said. "We can move you up, down, or sideways until you find the position you want, but I'd like to hang onto you."

"I'm enjoying my spot in receiving right now. The timing was right for me to do this type of job. I need the quiet since I'm still processing everything."

"Yeah, I'm sorry about the accident. Tony and Tommy were my second cousins. We used to play together all the time before they moved. I hated to hear about what happened."

"I hated it too," I said. We were both quiet for a few seconds. "You don't think this kind of thing will happen to you. Something just seems wrong about being a widow at twenty-three."

"Which one were you married to?"

"Tony. I called him Anthony."

"How long were you married?"

"A year. But we'd been together for four."

"Was he good to you?"

I sighed. "The best."

"Lulu's precious too. They're a good family."

"It's tough for her right now, but she'll get through it."

"I'm sure it's tough for both of you. I'm glad you have each other."

I smiled at him and stood up. "My break is almost over." I dusted my backside as he stood. He was standing close to me, towering over me like he must have been a foot taller. Maybe it wasn't that much, but he was a big guy and I stared up at him with a smile.

"I really appreciate the opportunity."

"No moving on, all right? Come to me if you want a new situation, don't go somewhere else."

I smiled and bowed a little. "I'm thankful to be here."

He used a finger to tilt my chin, forcing me to make eye contact. "Thank you for helping Lu," he said. "She's family and it means a lot that you're helping her."

"We're helping each other," I said.

Chapter 4

"Why don't you let people call you Lulu?" was the first thing I asked when I walked into the apartment after work that day.

The conversation I had with Dominic earlier was still fresh in my mind, and I could still hear him calling her that. He sounded so natural saying it and it was a good name for her.

"Gianni never called me that," she said, drawing me out of my thoughts. "He was pretty much the only one around here who didn't. Anyway, when we went out to Arizona, Vinny was the only one who ever called me that anymore, and little by little he just sort of switched over to calling me Laura. I don't know why I didn't want them saying Lulu. It just struck me wrong when I heard it. It's just because it's a happy name, I think."

"I thought it sounded good when people said it. It fits you."

"It used to."

"It will again one day."

She put her hand on mine. "I don't think I would have made it without you."

"It should be me who's saying that," I said. "You have all these people over here who love you. I talked to Dominic today, and he seemed willing to bend over backwards to make me comfortable at Nic's."

"You talked to Dominic? I was wondering when you'd meet him. He was such a precious little boy."

Laura knew he was wealthy, and I'd told her about his business, but she still had no concept of just how successful he was. She hadn't been to the store, and I could tell she wasn't processing the magnitude of his empire.

"I told him I wanted to learn how to take pictures and he said his love for photography was what got him started."

"Yeah he's been doing that since he was a little boy. His mom used to mail me some of the pictures he took. I think he won some kind of art show or a scholarship, or maybe both. He's always been special."

"It's nice to have people like him on your side, you know. He told me he'd do anything to make me comfortable there. You're lucky to have people like that looking out for you." I said.

"What did he tell you?"

"He just said for me to stay working for Nic's no matter what—said if I got tired of working in receiving he'd give me another job. He seemed like he wanted to do whatever to make me comfortable."

She smiled at me and squeezed my hand. "It makes my heart happy that you've found favor with him. This makes me feel so much better about dragging you all the way out here."

"I came because I wanted to."

36

"I know, sweetheart, but you knew deep down I needed you, and it makes me feel good that my people are looking after you."

"I needed you just as much," I said.

She smiled at me but I could tell she thought I was just being nice.

"I'm glad they're looking after me too," I said. "It's a good feeling, having someone like him on your side. He just seems so powerful, like he could help you out of any bind you got yourself in."

"He is powerful," she said. "He was powerful before the business, so you can just imagine."

"How so?" I asked.

"What do you mean?"

"You said he was powerful before he started his business. How so?"

"Oh, because he comes from a powerful family," she said. "The Russos are well-known around here. His dad is Big Willy Russo, and his uncles and granddad go way back on these streets."

I wanted to come out and ask if these guys were part of the mafia, but everything she'd said was vague enough that I'd feel bad if I assumed that and was wrong. I was in the middle of having that thought when someone pounded on the door with a heavy fist. I gasped and jumped and Laura looked at me with a curious expression as to who it could be. I shrugged.

"It must have been someone with the code because we didn't buzz anyone up," she said.

The mafia thoughts were fresh in my mind and I tried to think if I'd done anything wrong.

"I got a delivery for you Ms. Laura," we heard a man's voice say as we approached the door.

I reached up and peered through the peephole. "It's Mike," I said, reaching for the doorknob.

"Hi ya Ms. Rae," he said coming to stand in the apartment. "Ms. Laura," he added, nodding at her. "Sorry your box got a little wet," he said, handing me the package he was holding. The box was barely wet, like it had just started to sprinkle outside.

He took off his fedora and checked the top of it, smiling when he saw that it was barely wet too. He extended the hat in the direction of the box I was holding. "I knew the delivery guy down stairs. He was about to ring you, but I told him I had the code. I was coming up to tell you Frankie and Viv want to have you over for dinner tomorrow night."

I glanced at Laura and we both nodded. "Tell them we'll be there," she said.

"All right, that's good." He pointed at the package I was holding. "Enjoy."

I absentmindedly wondered if he somehow knew what was in it, but didn't think that was the case. Mike tipped his hat to us both before he left.

"What is it?" She asked as the door closed behind him.

"I was gonna ask you the same thing," I said.

"Well, what's it say?" she asked.

I turned the box around, inspecting it. I was perplexed to find that there were absolutely no markings on the thing—not a name, or address, or any clue of what was inside or who it was from.

I took it to the table where I set it down before using a key to cut the tape that was holding it closed. I started to open it, but then stopped and looked at her. "You don't think it's sketchy that it's not marked, do you?"

"No, Mike said he knew the guy carrying it."

I smiled as I continued opening the box. It was packaged with the same brown paper I often saw when I opened a box at work. My first thought when I saw it was that it might have come from Nic's, but I quickly passed that off. We both looked in curiously as I pulled out the top layer of brown paper.

There were a bunch of boxes that I instantly recognized from work. I wasn't a mathematician, but one glance into the box and I knew there was a lot of money involved. There was an envelope on top that was marked with my name.

Rae Milano

I stared down at it before glancing at Laura with a bewildered expression.

"Did someone send you a camera? Is that what this is?"

There were three boxes that were visible, and based on the size of the container, they were stacked two deep. I'd done enough research recently to know the level of equipment I was staring at.

"It seems that's the case, but I'm almost scared to investigate, because I'm already looking at a ton of money right here."

Her eyes got big. "Well, what are you waiting for? Open the letter and see what it's all about."

I was extremely skeptical that this was all for me. It was just too much. There had to be another explanation.

"It's got your name on it," she said, handing me the envelope. I opened the letter cautiously and read it out loud.

Rae, I'm glad we had the chance to meet today. Here are a few things to get you started taking pictures. I've included an assortment of my favorite lenses and look forward to finding out which one you like best. I think you'll really enjoy this set-up.

The letter wasn't over, but I paused and looked up at Laura. "Why would he do this?" I asked.

She shrugged. "Did you mention wanting it?"

"I mean, I might have casually said I'd like to get into it, but my goodness, I certainly didn't say I wanted him to do *this*." I sighed and focused my attention on the letter.

I've also included phones for yourself and Lulu.

I glanced up at her with wide eyes and put the letter down so I could dig in the box. I carefully took one of the lenses out and set it on the table. I peered into the box as I took a second lens off the top layer. I set it on the table as I looked into the box again. Sure enough, there were two small boxes that

40

contained the latest, greatest smartphone. I took one out and turned it over. "What's going on?" I asked.

"Just read the letter," she said.

I focused on the piece of paper, which was now shaking slightly.

I added the two of you to the same plan I provide for my managers at work. Calls, texting, and data are unlimited so don't worry about overages.

I glanced up at her in disbelief, but then focused on the letter again.

The phones have been activated, but you need to use them to call the service provider and confirm a few things. I get a good price on the service with my group plan. It's my pleasure to take care of this, so please let me. I'm sure you'll be a manager soon enough, anyway. I am going to London for a couple of weeks, but my mom says she wants to do dinner with you and Lulu soon. Get ready for my mom. She's a hugger.

I laughed and glanced at Laura. She smiled. "Maria Russo will squeeze the living daylights out of you," she said.

Oh, and by the way, tell Lu she doesn't have to worry about you while you're at work. I already warned every man in the building that you're off limits. I told the guys at the deli too, just for good measure. Tell her everyone loves you and is keeping their eye out for you over here. Enjoy your new toys. My number has already been programed into your phones if you need anything.

41

Take care,
Dominic

"This is an unbelievably generous gift," I said. Taking the boxes out one by one. There were two photography books on the bottom, and I thumbed through them distractedly.

"You must have really made an impression on him today."

"I don't know how," I said. "I was just sitting on a curb in my work uniform."

"Well you must have made an impression somehow. What'd you guys talk about?"

"I'm trying to remember our conversation. I told him I wanted to get into taking pictures but I just barely mentioned it. I also barely mentioned the fact that I didn't have a phone. I can't believe he sent these. You see the red ring around these lenses?" I asked, pointing at the picture of the lens that was printed on the box.

She nodded.

"This basically means that this baby takes amazing pictures. This camera will take pictures by itself. All I have to do is strap it on my shoulder and walk by something and I've got quality photos."

She watched me excitedly inspect everything with great pride that part of her family had done something so thoughtful for me.

"I wonder why he's going to London," she said.

"He's looking at opening a store there," I said. "A guy I work with named Matt told me that earlier today after he saw me talking to Dominic. He didn't tell me Dominic was planning a trip, but he must have known it because he told me about the new store. He talked my ear off about Dominic for about an hour while we broke down boxes this afternoon."

"I'll have to call Maria and tell her what a doll her son is."

"You can call her from your new phone."

"I need to get her number programmed into it," she said.

Both of us shut off our cellphone service before we left Arizona. She bought a prepaid phone for our trip, but we only used it to talk to her family on the way up here and had it for emergencies, of course.

She and I spent the remainder of the evening programming our new phones and checking them out. We took about a hundred selfies together before she settled on one that she'd send to Dominic as a thank you.

I still hadn't decided what I'd do to thank him. I wasn't used to this type of no-strings-attached generosity, and I kept feeling like I should get on some kind of payment plan to reimburse him. Laura assured me a hundred times that I should just accept the gift for what it was, and I did my best to take her advice.

She had a conversation with Dominic's mom later that evening, but I could only hear half of it, so I went to my nook to crack into the camera and lenses now that I had time to really inspect everything and read the instructions. Laura went into her room at 10PM, and I stayed up till 2AM playing with my camera. I skimmed through the books he included and used my new phone to watch YouTube videos about the camera and how to use it.

I went to bed still feeling amazed at the generosity of her family.

Chapter 5

Laura and I went to Frankie and Vivian's for dinner the following evening. Their apartment was only three blocks from ours, but was on a whole other level. I'd been there one time with Laura when she went to clean while Frankie and Vivian weren't home.

Tonight would be the first time I'd meet Vivian, and I felt somewhat nervous. Laura said we'd get along fine, and I knew that was true, but it seemed like I was meeting new people every time I turned around, and I still got a little anxious.

The doorman recognized us and sent us upstairs with a warm greeting. Our building didn't have a doorman, and I smiled at the fanciness of being welcomed by a uniformed representative.

A woman I assumed was Vivian smiled broadly when she opened the door and instantly reached out to bring Laura into her arms. "I can't believe I'm just now getting to see you and you're right down the street!" she said. "We should have already had a party."

"Oh, definitely no parties," Laura said, hugging her back as we came to stand in the entryway.

"You must be Rae. I'm Aunt Viv, you precious love. I've heard so many great things about you!" She pulled me into her arms and gave me a tight hug, and then she pulled back and regarded me sweetly before pinching my cheek. "What an absolute stunner!" she said, looking at Laura with wide eyes. "Frankie told me she was a little blonde angel, but she is just a sight! Who'd she belong to?" she asked, taking me into her arms for another squeeze.

"Tony," Laura said. I looked at Laura to see if the candid question would affect her, but she seemed unruffled. "She's as good to me as she was to my boy," she said, stoically.

"You're lucky for that," Vivian said. She was extremely touchy feely. She had her hands all over us, giving us both pats and rubs, but somehow it wasn't intrusive. "I know it's been hard, honey, I can't imagine what you've been through, but you have a little angel with you, don't you?"

"I sure do," Laura said. "I don't know what I'd do if—"

"What's taking you broads so long?" we heard a man's voice yell.

"We're coming!" Viv shouted. "Give me a second! I haven't seen Lu in a million years!" Viv focused her attention on Laura again and rubbed her shoulder. "You look absolutely beautiful by the way. You haven't changed a bit, honey. I should have told you that when you first came in." Viv was on the verge of tears as she stared at Laura, and it was obvious that she loved and missed her very much. I couldn't help but take note that it was the first time Laura let someone call her Lu.

46

"Are you ladies just gonna stand by the door all night?" Frankie asked, coming around the corner with his arms out expecting hugs.

"Hey Frankie," Laura said, hugging him.

"Hey gorgeous," he said. He looked at Vivian as he took me into his arms. "And how's about this one, huh?"

"I know, right?" Vivian said. "Tony knew how to pick 'em."

"Yes he did," Laura said, smiling sweetly at me.

All three of them stood there and stared at me. Laura and Vivian both looked like they were on the verge of tearing up, but thankfully it didn't seem like it was out of sadness, but rather happiness caused by the reunion.

"Where'd you get that light hair?" he asked, reaching up to gently tug on a lock of my hair.

I had dirty blonde hair that was just curly enough for me not to fight it. I usually let it dry naturally and the curls hung in loose waves. "My dad, I think," I said smiling.

"Whatta ya mean you think?" Frankie asked, confused.

Laura reached up and backhanded him on the arm. It made a loud slapping sound, and he gave her an injured expression. "She didn't know her father," Laura said.

"I'm sorry, sweetheart," he said, shamefaced. "I didn't know."

"It's fine," I said, giving him a reassuring smile. "I never met him, but apparently I have his hair..." I hesitated. "...and his name. My grandma raised me, but my mom made her promise to name me Rae after my dad—only his was spelled R-A-Y like guy's spell it."

"Well your grandma must have done something right. Lu goes on and on about you, and she has good taste." Frankie called her Lu even though he'd already been warned, and again, she didn't correct him. For whatever reason, this was a dose of encouragement that covered me like a warm blanket. It was the first time I felt like there might be a light at the end of the tunnel.

"Thank you," I said.

"I don't know what we're doing standing in here," he said. "Take your shoes off and come get comfortable."

Laura and I slipped out of our shoes and followed Frankie and Viv into the living room. Frankie continued into the kitchen, but us girls took a seat on the couch.

"Does he need help in there?" Laura asked.

"No, the lasagna is baking and we already made the salad. He's just too antsy to come sit down."

"Mike said he saw one of Nic's boys bringing you a package yesterday," Frankie said from the kitchen. He sounded like he was straining when he spoke. I glanced his way to see that he was peering into the oven, watching dinner bake. I figured Laura would respond to his statement, so I just stayed quiet.

"Dominic Russo is the most generous man on the planet," Laura said. "After you of course, Frankie."

Frankie laughed. "I guess he sent you a welcome present or something?"

"He got us phones," she said.

"I thought you had a phone."

"I had a little prepaid, but Rae didn't have one at all, and he sent us these amazing little phones that are basically mini computers."

Frankie stood and stretched his hands onto the cabinet, looking at us. "What service are you gonna use?" he asked. "Viv and I could probably get you a good deal if you wanna jump on our family plan."

"Nic's taking care of it," she said. "He said he'd just put us on the same plan he gets for his managers."

"That was extremely generous," Viv said. She said it quietly, and Frankie took that as a hint that they didn't want to yell across the apartment anymore. He was antsy again anyway. He turned to dig in the fridge and the three of us continued the conversation.

"I already called Maria to tell her what a good boy she raised," Laura said. "And that's not all. He sent a real nice camera for Rae."

"Really?" Vivian asked. She asked it with an expression that told me she might think he did it

49

because he was a guy and I was a girl and maybe he was attracted to me in that way. It was the first time I ever even considered such a thing, and in that split second, I tried to remember our conversation—tried to remember if it felt like that at all.

The answer was no.

He was incredibly respectful of me being Anthony's wife, and didn't seem at all like he had any ulterior motives. Not to mention the fact that he was way out of my league. In fact, a *few* leagues separated Dominic Russo and me—especially with my baggage. I smiled internally at the thought of Vivian raising her eyebrows like the gift could have been romantic.

"He and I had a conversation where I told him I wanted to get into taking photos," I explained. "He knew I couldn't afford the kind of stuff he sells at his store, and I think he's just the type of guy that does random kind things like that."

Vivian closed her eyes and shook her head, smiling. "I love that boy," she said. "Isn't he precious?"

"I'm taking this out, Viv!" Frankie yelled from the kitchen. He was nervously watching the dish bubble through the oven's glass window.

"The timer's set, honey, but do whatever you think."

Without further ado, Frankie opened the oven and carefully removed the steaming hot pan with oven mitts.

Dinner was delicious, and our hosts were more than gracious. Viv made us promise to catch up with her again some evenings since she worked at a jewelry store during the day and was always gone when Laura came to clean.

**

Laura and I kept our promise to see Viv regularly. It had been two weeks since we first had dinner at their house, and we'd seen her twice since then. She kept asking when it'd be okay to have a girls' get-together, but Laura just wasn't ready for that yet.

Things were still hard for me, but day-by-day it was getting better. I knew the same was true for Laura even though she'd never admit such a thing. She claimed she was still miserable, but I saw her smiles grow more genuine with each passing day. We both still struggled to understand why we'd lived through such a tragedy, but we were slightly less obsessed by it every day.

I dove into photography as a way of coping. I'd had my camera for two weeks, and officially took it everywhere I went. I was a total nerd—researching and taking photos with every spare second I had. I brought a computer from Arizona with me, and every night I uploaded hundreds of photos I'd taken that day. I shot sidewalks, architecture, graffiti, statues, red lights, trees, animals, and whatever else I thought might be interesting.

I started studying great photographers and had become familiar enough with some of their work that I'd experiment with replicating their photos. Every night I'd show Laura my best ones, and she was extremely encouraging, telling me I had good instincts and things like that.

We had a big print center upstairs at work where I just had 8x10's of my favorites printed. They were currently sitting on my desk, and I was excited to show them to Laura. I loved seeing them on paper. It was different than a screen—better.

I only got ten of them because I was still living on the small change I brought from Arizona. In fact, today was the first time I'd get a paycheck. Just as I had that thought, Debbie came by receiving to notify me that she sent an email with my paystub details, but that the money would direct deposit by midnight per my request. The others heard her talking to me and gave her a hard time about not getting them the money before midnight. She was laughing when she left.

Out of sheer curiosity I checked my email. The math was relatively simple. I knew roughly what I was making before taxes and insurance, but wasn't totally clear on what I'd have left after those got taken out. I didn't have health insurance taken out of my check when I worked at the coffee shop because Anthony and I were covered through the dealership. Anyway, I was expecting about forty percent of my paycheck to go out the window by the time it was all said and done.

I stared at the screen, unable to read the spreadsheet correctly. The numbers were too high. My hourly wage was off. It was significantly higher than the rate at which I'd been hired, and I sighed knowing I'd have to jump through some hoops to get it corrected and it'd probably delay getting my check.

I scanned the whole page. Everything was wrong. The personal information was all correct, and so were the number of hours, but *everything else* was messed up.

"I need to run upstairs and talk to Debbie about my paycheck," I said as I walked back into the common area.

"No problem," Matt said, without even looking at me.

I walked upstairs with my phone in my hand so that I could access my email. Debbie saw me through the wall of glass when I approached her office and she smiled, waving me in.

"What's the matter?" she asked, noticing I wasn't smiling.

"I think my paycheck's messed up," I said. I sat in the chair facing her desk.

She shook her head. "I don't think so," she said. "I looked at it before I sent it."

"It's supposed to be way less than it is," I said. "Or maybe I'm just reading it wrong."

She started clicking away on her keyboard and then turned her monitor to show me what she was looking at.

I peered over her desk to view it. "Yeah, see?" I pointed at the box for hourly wage—the one that was fifty percent higher than the price I agreed on when I signed up for this job.

She looked at me with a nod.

"It's more than I'm supposed to be making."

"I know. Dominic had me make that adjustment before he left for his trip."

"That's a big adjustment," I said in disbelief. "That's too much of an adjustment."

She smiled and shrugged. "I just do what he tells me to do. I thought you two worked it out."

"I had no idea. Are you telling me that's correct?"

She nodded.

I was overwhelmed, and almost forgot to ask, but then remembered. "How do I figure out how much comes out for insurance?"

She giggled as she shook her head. "I should have known he didn't talk to you about that either."

"About what?"

"Dominic's not taking insurance out of your check."

I squinted at her, feeling like I couldn't believe my ears. "Do I still get coverage?" I asked.

She smiled like it was sweet for me to even ask such a thing. "Of course you do. Don't quote me on this, but I think he's planning on covering your mother-in-law too. He had his assistant set it up, so I'm not sure, but I heard him mention it."

It was too much. I simply couldn't believe the way Laura's family stuck by her. I knew Dominic's kindness toward me was aimed at Laura, and I marveled that such families existed in the world. I was quiet while I thought about these things.

"So everything seems right on this end," Debbie said, with a matter of fact smile like our meeting was over.

Chapter 6

"I got a huge raise and they're not taking insurance out of my check," I said when I opened the door to the apartment.

Laura was standing in the small kitchen and she cocked her head at me. "Say it again, slower this time," she said.

"Dominic's paying me way more than we agreed on, and he's covering insurance too. It's not coming out of my check. I held up my phone as a symbol of my paycheck. "It's way more than I thought it'd be," I said, unable to stop a smile. I opened the email and walked my phone over to Laura. I set it on the counter and she squinted down at it.

She instantly pinched the screen, trying to make it bigger then proceeded to inspect it for several seconds before looking at me. "You're kidding me!"

I shook my head. "I made sure with my boss. She said Dominic told her to adjust it. She acted surprised I didn't already know about it."

"We're going to have to do something to thank him."

"I already sent him a card for the camera and phones. I don't even know if he got that yet. Is he back in town?"

"You'd know that before I would," she said. "I'll write a letter thanking him too."

I didn't dare tell her what Debbie said about her insurance. We'd just have to see if anything ever came of that. "I got my prints today," I said instead. I took my backpack off and set it on the counter so I could dig for the envelope containing the photos. I handed it to Laura.

She ran her finger across the envelope where it said *Nic's Prints* with stripes of blues and yellows and his signature logo of a Polaroid camera. "It's amazing to see his name printed on the envelope like that," she said.

We looked at my photos, and one by one she told me what she liked about them. I learned a lot by hearing her feedback. It was nice to hear what struck people when they looked at your work. I put the photos back in the envelope and slid it back into my backpack. We were silent for several seconds, both thinking.

"I can't believe your paycheck," she said.

"Wanna go out for dinner?"

She smiled. It was a good, genuine smile that made me happy. She was glad Dominic was being nice for my sake and I was glad he was being nice for hers. It wasn't about the money so much as the happy feeling we both got on each other's behalf.

It was a good night.

We went to a place she remembered from when she lived there before. It was a steak house with quote-unquote the best steaks on the planet. It said it right on the door, and after I ate one, I might have just believed it. They didn't have a wide variety on their menu. Basically, you just chose how big of a steak you wanted and what sides you wanted with it. They did one thing and did it well, and we went to bed full that evening.

I laid in bed considering texting Dominic for his generosity, but I had never text him before and thought it might be odd to do so for the first time at 10PM. Instead, I decided to gather a few of my favorite prints along with a thank you note and deliver it to him the next day—that way he could see I'd been using the camera.

I chose my three favorites.

One was a bulldog that was randomly tied to a lamppost outside the deli the other day. He had on a spike collar and was just about the most photogenic thing on the planet.

The second was a colorful chalk hopscotch game with a kid's legs and feet hopping. You couldn't see the whole kid, just from the knees down, and her Converse were positioned in a perfect hopping pose at the top of the photo.

The third was Laura. It was a black and white portrait of her. I captured the pain she'd been through, and the photo was undeniably compelling. Laura didn't think it was flattering of herself, but she liked it because it was a true representation of her feelings over the last month.

I'd taken some photos of her smiling. I knew I could get one of those printed, or just choose another from the prints I had, but I chose to give the melancholy portrait to Dominic. I packaged the three 8x10's in a big envelope along with a note.

Dominic,

I don't know what to say. I assumed my paycheck was a mistake, and couldn't believe when Debbie told me it wasn't. I know this is for Laura's sake, which touches my heart. She is so fortunate to have such a family, and I'm honored and blessed that I was taken into the fold. The raise and insurance were unexpected and so very appreciated. Rest assured that I'll do my best to earn the rate you're paying me. I'm stunned by your generosity and can't tell you how thankful I am.

Sincerely,

Rae

The next morning when I got to work, I gave the envelope to Debbie same as I did with the other thank you card, which Dominic might or might not have gotten by now. When I gave it to her, she told me Dominic was back from his trip.

For whatever reason that made me slightly nervous. I almost chickened out of giving him the photos, but that would mean taking the envelope off Debbie's desk and saying never mind. Basically, I chickened out of chickening out, and now Dominic was gonna see my pictures whether I liked it or not.

None of them were inspired by other people's work, but I was still nervous about what he'd think of them. I tried not to think about it, and had done a pretty good job of it until Debbie came down to receiving to tell me Dominic wanted to see me in his office. I felt like I was being called to the principal's office, and trembled all the way up to the fifth floor. Before Debbie came to me with these instructions, I had no idea Dominic even had an office in this building. I rode to the fifth floor feeling anxious about what I'd find when I got there.

There was a well-dressed woman sitting at a desk that faced the elevator. Facing her in my uniform shirt made me feel way underdressed and a little self-conscious. I smiled as confidently as I could at her.

She smiled back. "How can I help you?" she asked.

"I'm supposed to see Dominic."

"Are you Rae?"

"Yes."

"His office is all the way at the end." She pointed to her right down a hallway. "I'll let him know you're coming down."

I heard her warning him of my approach as I walked toward his office, and his door swung open before I made it there. "Come in," he said, smiling broadly at me.

It had been a couple of weeks since I saw him, and for whatever reason, his smile was like a breath of fresh air.

"What happened in the two weeks I was gone?"

I was in the process of following him to his desk when he asked, and I waited till I sat down to speak.

I cleared my throat. "What do you mean?" was all I could come up with.

Instead of sitting behind his desk like I thought he'd do, he stood near me and sat on the edge of his desk, crossing his legs in front of him casually. He turned to reach for some papers that were sitting on the desk and when he faced me again I realized they were my pictures.

"How did you learn to take these pictures in two weeks? Did you take these?" He held them up, and I nodded. "Do you have photo editing software?"

"Just the program that came with the computer. I don't know much about it, but I'm trying stuff with different filters."

"Rae, I'm not just saying this... these are amazing. I love your work."

I wasn't able to contain a smile. "Don't give me too much credit," I said. "That camera could take pictures by itself."

He scoffed. "That's false and you know it. You have a special gift, Rae. We're gonna put it to the test."

"What? What's that mean?"

He was amused at my jumpiness I could tell. I narrowed my eyes at him, and his smile broadened.

"Next month I'm going to hold the first annual employee photo contest. I have over two hundred employees, and most of them are into photography. I can't believe I haven't thought of it before. You'll have to send a digital file or an 8x10 to me by November first. I'll hang the photos on the east wall. Customers will have the chance to place their vote at checkout using a number system."

"I sure hope you're not doing any of this because of me. There are far better photographers than me down stairs, and that's just in shipping and receiving."

"I'm having the contest. You don't have to win, but you have to enter. If you don't turn anything in, I'll just enter one of these."

I giggled. "Which one would you choose?"

"Laura probably, but the hopscotch—wow. I wish I could put all three, but I'll only be able to do one entry per person or else we'd never be able to display them all."

I dropped my gaze. "I hope I got across how very thankful I am for everything," I said. "I'm baffled by your kindness.

"You're family," he said simply. "I'm happy to do it, and we don't need to mention it again."

I could see him swivel to put the photos on his desk. He crossed his arms when he turned back around, but all of this I saw out of my periphery since I was looking down. "London went well," he said.

I glanced up and met his eye. "I'm glad to hear it."

"I'll be opening a location there next year if all goes as planned."

"Oh, that's exciting. I've never been there."

"I took some pictures if you'd like to see them sometime."

"I'd love to."

"Now?"

I smiled, and felt myself blushing. "I told Matt I'd be back down there as soon as—"

"Rae."

"Yeah?"

"Do you know who I am?"

"Yeah."

"Who?"

"Dominic."

"That's right. And do you know whose name is written on the outside of the building?"

"Yours."

"Yep. That means I own the place, which also means I make the rules around here." He was smiling the whole time he was talking, which made me regard him with narrowed eyes. I could tell he enjoyed pushing my buttons.

"I'd love to see your pictures Mr. Russo," I said.

He smiled. "That's better."

I stayed in his office for a good while, looking at the hundreds of photos he took in London. He let me sit in his chair and use his computer while he used his phone to take care of some email.

"You're an excellent photographer," I said when I finished looking at the last photograph on the camera roll.

He set his phone on the desk and leaned back, regarding me with a smile. "Oh yeah?" he asked. "Think I could take you in the contest?"

"Definitely," I said, without hesitation. "No doubt you could take me. Are you entering?"

"No."

"Why not? You'd win."

"It's against the rules for me to enter."

"I thought you just said you make the rules around here."

"I do," he said smiling. "And that's one of my rules. I can't enter."

I gave him another teasing scowl. "You're trying to take it easy on me," I said, "but just so you know, I could take you even if you *did* enter."

He laughed. "I love it. I might have to just to accept the challenge."

"Let's do it," I said, smiling.

"I'll even let you pick what photo I submit," he said. He pointed at the monitor. "Go ahead and pick from the ones you just looked at."

I sighed. "There you go again."

"What?"

"You're trying to take it easy on me. You can't let *me* pick your entry. I could choose the worst one on purpose."

He gave me an offended look. "There aren't any bad ones in there."

I laughed. "You're not tricking me into letting you let me win, mister," I said pointing at him. "I'm just playing," I quickly amended. "That implies that I think I could make it past everyone on the main floor, which I don't."

"I'm glad you gave me the idea for the contest," he said. "I think it'll be a hit with the customers."

"Thanks for liking my photos, and for the camera in the first place." I glanced at the clock and gasped when I saw that it was nearly time for me to clock out. The main floor stayed open late, but shipping and receiving shut down at five.

I sprang out of the chair, and Dominic just stared at me with that same amused grin I seemed to evoke in him.

"I emailed Debbie while you were looking at the photos. She had your things brought up. They're at Bridgette's desk. Matt's clocking you out when the rest of them leave at five."

"I feel bad like they're gonna be mad at me or something."

He cocked his head at me. "Who's the boss?"

"You."

"So why are you trying to impress Matt in receiving."

"I'm not, I just don't want—"

"Don't worry about it. Nobody's mad. Everybody loves you down there."

I smiled shyly. "I loved your photos," I said. "I'd like to ask you some questions sometime when you get the—"

"Now."

"Like right now?"

"Yep."

I couldn't hold back a grin. I stayed in Dominic's office for the next two hours. I asked him questions and he gave me insightful answers. I learned more about photography in that two hours than I had in two weeks of extensive research, and I left feeling overwhelmed by how much I had to learn, but excited at the same time to try some new things.

Chapter 7

Dominic emailed all the employees of Nic's the very next day announcing the contest. Each person would be allowed one submission. Entries were due by November first. Halfway through the month, they'd announce the top ten. The slate would be clean at that point, and the remainder of the month would feature only the ten finalists.

The winner would be announced the first week of December and would receive a check for a thousand dollars. The second place prize was five hundred and the third was three hundred. I had almost two weeks to decide which photo I'd enter, and that time snuck past me so quickly that I could hardly believe it was already time to turn in our entries.

Dominic helped me narrow it down to two photos. He'd been extremely helpful the last couple of weeks, answering my questions and giving advice when I asked. I didn't call him or anything—I just relied on seeing him around, which had happened quite a bit since he'd been in the store a lot lately.

I showed him my five favorite photos, and he chose his top two. I went with one I'd taken of a street act at the subway station. It was a photo of a one-man band. I took it from lying on the ground near the guy's feet and looking up at him with a really cool fisheye lens that Dominic included in my kit. There were no rules on whether the print had to be black and white or in color, so I opted for color since his clothes and instruments were interesting and bright. I went back and forth between that one and the portrait of Laura, which was Dominic's other choice. He loved them both, but it boiled down to the one I thought might get the most votes. Dominic didn't enter, but it wasn't because he didn't have a winning photograph in his portfolio; he just wanted it to be about his employees.

He came down to receiving the afternoon the photos were due. "Entries to the photo contest are due by five today," he said, coming into the common area.

"Everyone who's entering from down here already turned theirs in," Matt said. "How many entered so far?"

"Over a hundred last time I checked," Dominic said. He glanced around the room with an easy smile, and stopped when his eyes landed on me. "Which one did you go with?"

"The street act."

He smiled like he thought that might be a good choice.

"Mine's a picture of my little boy's feet," Matt said. "Did you see it?"

Dominic shifted his attention to Matt. "I didn't have the chance to go through them all yet," he said. "I'm sure I'll love it, though. I'm excited about it. I'm glad you guys entered."

"Mine's a picture of my dog, but it's really cool. You'll have to see it," Hannah said.

"I can't wait to see them all," Dominic said. "We'll have a crew working on the display all night tomorrow and they'll be on the wall by Thursday morning. Don't forget you guys each get a vote."

***

For the next two weeks, everyone who visited the main showroom floor could see the array of beautiful photographs. Some of them were amazing on their own, and others weren't, but seeing them all displayed together made them all seem appealing. I passed through there to look at them about every other time I worked, and it seemed like my favorite changed each time.

"Did you vote yet?" I heard a man's voice ask from behind me. I knew it was Dominic. I recognized his voice.

"I'm going to vote now. It's so hard for me to choose."

He gave me a confused look. "Well, obviously you should vote for yourself."

I laughed. "I can't do that. It's embarrassing."

"No it's not. It's a thousand dollars." He paused. "I voted for you."

"I can't believe you get to vote."

"I can't believe you forgot I make the rules," he said smiling. He gestured toward one of the cash registers. "You need to go vote. The top ten are chosen tonight."

"I know. That's why I'm standing here looking," I said. "I'm trying to decide."

He leveled me with a stare, and speaking in hushed tones, he said, "You punch the number into the keypad. The cashier can't see who you vote for. Just go over there and press 8-6. You know you want to."

He was so right; I did want to. "You promise they can't see?" I asked.

He smiled. "Yes."

"Yes they can see?"

"No, yes I promise they can't."

"Laura came in the other day and bought a pack of gum so she could vote," I said. "I think Frankie and Viv did too." (Laura had actually bought three different packs of gum since the contest started.) "Can you see who's winning so far?" I asked. I knew it sounded desperate, and I really didn't want to ask, but I couldn't stop myself—it just came out before I could do anything about it. I began blushing right when I said it, so I pretended to dig in my bag.

"I can peek if I want to, yes," he said. I could hear the smile in his voice even though I wasn't looking at him.

I glanced up when I said, "Did you peek?"

His face broke into a broad grin, flashing his white teeth. "Yes."

I gave him an exasperated look. "Did I get some votes?"

"Well, you just told me about five, plus yours, that'll make six."

"That's all I got? Five votes?"

"I didn't say that."

I gave him a look that begged him to be straight with me. "Is it even worth voting for myself, or am I not even close to the top ten?"

"Do you want me to tell you?" he asked. I could tell by the way he said it that he would if I wanted him to.

"I don't think so," I said. "It doesn't seem fair that I'd get to know ahead of everyone else."

"That's not the reason I'm hesitating. I'd just hate to tell you one thing, and have something else happen by the time voting closes. I think there are probably other people buying gum between now and then if you know what I mean." He paused. "I could just give you the win if I wanted to."

"Don't you dare," I said with wide eyes.

He laughed. "I wouldn't. But I could. Hey, before you go vote for number 86, I had two other things I wanted to talk to you about."

I gave him a curious glance, and he continued.

"I had someone track down your one-man band the other day to bring him a print and tell him the photo was being displayed. I thought he might want to come by and see it. I hope you don't mind."

I smiled at his thoughtfulness. "I don't mind at all," I said. "Thank you for doing that."

"The other thing was, I wanted to ask if you'd be willing to do a photo shoot with me."

"Like you need my help on a shoot… or are you asking to take my picture?" I instantly regretted saying that last part, but there was nothing I could do to take it back.

"Neither. I need you to take my picture for an interview I'm doing with a magazine."

I let out an uncontrollable laugh. "No." I said, as if that were the only reasonable thing for me to say.

He just looked at me like he was serious.

"I'm not ready for that," I said, stating the obvious.

"Yes you are," he said. "I have a few ideas for it. We'll work together on it."

"So basically all you need me to do is push the button?"

He shrugged. "If you want to look at it like that."

"I definitely don't want any sort of credit, not that I assumed you were gonna give me—what magazine?"

He smiled at my ramblings. "Forbes."

"Oh, no. No way. I'm definitely not ready for that."

"Yes you are. You're off tomorrow. Can you make it to my house at say, 11AM?"

I stared at him, hoping he'd take pity on my insecurities, but answered with, "I guess so if you're sure I can't mess it up."

"You can't. I'll see you then. I'll send a driver to your building at 10:30. Bring Lulu if you want."

"I might do that if you don't mind. She doesn't have work tomorrow either, and we've heard how cool your house is."

"If you think she'll come with you, I'll tell my mom to come too. I don't think she's seen Lu yet."

"Not many people have besides Frankie and Viv. She still doesn't feel like the person she used to be."

"That's understandable," he said. "She lost everything in that accident."

"I know," I said. "They were sort of all I had too, but her pain has to be worse than mine. I can't imagine."

"Do you ever think about what it would have been like if you'd have been pregnant?"

It was a question no one ever dared ask me, but I answered without hesitation. "All the time," I said. "I feel a lot of guilt over that. Anthony wanted to start a family, and I thought we should wait a little longer. If I would have agreed to start trying, Laura might have a piece of her son."

"Do you regret it for yourself—that you don't have a piece of Anthony to hold onto?"

"I did at first, I think. The sadness of losing him was so great that I tortured myself with guilt about it."

"And now?"

"I don't know," I said feeling bad for even thinking about it. "It would have been hard trying to start over with a baby on the way."

He studied me for a few seconds, and I thought he was going to say more about me not having Anthony's baby, but he didn't.

"I'll send a driver for you and Lu in the morning," he said instead.

"That's fine as long as I'm just pushing the button."

He smiled at me as he turned to walk away. "86," he said from over his shoulder.

I shook my head at him like he was being silly, but then preceded to march my booty to the register and type the numbers 8-6 into the keypad.

Laura came with me to Dominic's house the next morning. The driver brought us to an apartment building about twelve blocks away. He told us to go up to the twentieth floor to apartment 203, so we did as instructed.

"I think he's got two places," Laura said as we rode up the elevator.

"That makes since, because Frankie mentioned koi ponds and gardens, and I can't imagine where they'd be in a place like this, unless he was on the roof."

"I'm sure he has roof access," Laura said, pointing to the elevator buttons to indicate that we were riding to the top floor. "But I think he has a house outside the city. We'll have to ask him."

Maria Russo will squeeze the ever-living daylights out of you, and she did it to both Laura and me when we walked into Dominic's place. It was way bigger than our apartment, but still not quite what I'd expect from someone about to appear in Forbes Magazine. It was clean and masculine, and definitely nice, but it wasn't gaudy or overboard like I pictured from a camera mogul.

"I can't believe what a little blonde angel she is," Maria said. She was talking to Laura, but staring straight at me. "She's just as cute as can be." She looked at Dominic. "She's a cutie, isn't she?"

"Yes she is," he agreed. "I should be taking her picture instead."

I stared down at the compliment. It was the first time he'd ever said something like that about me, and I felt shy and embarrassed about it.

"Tony knew how to pick 'em," Laura said.

"He sure did, Lu," Maria said. She was no longer correcting people when they called her that, and I smiled internally at the sound of it.

"Should we get started?" I asked, looking at Dominic. I was anxious to get alone with him because I wanted to see if he'd tell me who the finalists were. Voting had already closed, and the top ten were going to be revealed Monday, but I thought he might tell me if I wanted to know. I didn't want to ask in front of Laura and Maria, but I was excited to find out.

He had two studio strobes set up on the far side of his living room near a brick wall, and he pointed to that area when I asked if he was ready to get started.

"We're working right there," he said. "We can make them go get a cup of coffee if you'd rather work alone."

"It doesn't matter to me," I said, feeling awkward.

"We'll get a cup of coffee and give you two the chance to get some work done," Maria said.

"I was telling Rae I thought you had a house outside the city somewhere."

"Oh he does," Maria said, answering for Dominic. "It's so nice out there. You should really come sometime."

"I assumed Rae would bring Lu to the Thanksgiving feast," he said.

I'd heard about the annual Thanksgiving feast—I knew it was something everyone looked forward to, but I had no idea it was at Dominic's house.

"I thought it was all your employees plus one," I said suddenly perplexed.

"It is."

"That's like four hundred people."

"It's a bit of a drive. Not everyone can make it, and some come alone, but we usually have about two hundred."

"You have a house that two hundred people can fit into?"

He smiled. "It's tight, but yeah, we fit."

"Dominic's house was built for entertaining," Maria said. "The previous owners had house parties all the time. The Thanksgiving feast is a huge hit every year. He hires a band and other entertainers, and feeds everyone a gourmet meal."

"It's not that big of a deal." He looked at his mom. "I don't want to get her hopes up. It's a big house, but it's not an amusement park or anything."

"Frankie said it had a bowling alley and three koi ponds."

"The previous owners were bowlers," he said humbly. "And it's just two lanes. The koi ponds, however, were my idea."

I smiled, but didn't know what to say.

"I'm excited to see it," Laura said.

"We could have done this shoot out there, but I didn't want to take up too much of your time this morning. Like I said, the trip's about an hour."

"We should let them get started," Maria said. "Oh, were you gonna tell her?"

"Tell her what?" Dominic asked.

"What you were telling me before they came in," Maria said.

"She probably doesn't want to hear," he said, looking at me.

"Hear what?" I asked. I figured they might be talking about the contest and I was already buzzing with nerves.

"That you made the top ten," Dominic said, casually.

"I did?" I asked with wide eyes.

He smiled. "Yes."

I squealed and instinctually reached out to hug him. I gave him a quick squeeze. He was as hard as a rock, much firmer to the touch than Anthony was, and my first thought was that he must work out a lot. I quickly let him go.

"Did I really make the top ten?" I asked.

"Yes," he said, smiling broadly.

"No cheating?" I asked.

He held his hands up in surrender. "No cheating."

I squealed again. Laura came over for a hug. She and Maria were both delighted at my excitement and congratulated me on their way out.

Chapter 8

Dominic walked me through the process of photographing someone in a studio setting. He had everything prepped, and was perfectly willing to explain the tools and their function as we went along. I'd never worked with a strobe (the big lights on a stand with an umbrella), and he gave me the beginner's version of how to use a light meter.

He also told me what to say to draw a certain emotion or pose from him, and then he'd wait for me to ask for it. I was really nervous at first, but settled into it quickly on account of his laid-back approach to the whole thing. Basically, he knew what sort of photos he wanted to take, and he just allowed me to be the instrument he used to get them.

I learned so much in the process. I was a hands-on type of person, and was so grateful that Dominic was so generous with his equipment and advice.

Something else happened during the shoot, though.

Taking Dominic's picture was eye opening on so many levels, and I'm not just talking about photography skills. Staring at him through the lens made me look at his face differently.

I knew it was way too early to be attracted to another man only a couple months after I lost Anthony, but I caught myself feeling nervous butterflies as I looked at his face through the lens. I reprimanded myself internally and tried to focus, but I'd become increasingly distracted by his dark, handsome features. His jaw was dusted with some dark stubble, and the lines of his cheekbones and nose were masculine and defined.

I swallowed against the growing sense of dread that I was going to start having trouble ignoring my attraction to his face.

"You okay?" he asked, noticing me staring into the camera intensely.

I jumped back and looked up to regard him face to face. "Me? Fine. I'm good. It's all good. You're easy to take pictures of. I was just thinking about what an easy subject you were."

"I don't want to be easy, Rae." I gave him a questioning glance and he continued, "I don't want you to just focus the camera and push a button. I want you to take a picture that represents me."

"That's too much pressure," I said.

"No it's not." He gestured at the camera. "Take it off the tripod."

I did as he said, trying my best not to be clumsy with it.

"I'll sit here with my eyes closed so I can't see what you're doing. Look at me from different angles and with different lighting. Take a photo and look at it on the screen, studying where the lights are falling on my face. Be mindful of shadows. Notice how they change when I shift. I'll just sit here for a minute while you try some new angles. Let me know if you want me to reposition and I will."

At that, he leaned on his hand for support and closed his eyes.

I was shy at first, but he just sat there with his eyes closed comfortably, and soon I got into trying different angles. I snapped some pictures, reviewed them, and moved around, trying new positions.

At first things were very clinical. I was nervous about moving around him, and approached it with nothing more than a photographer's eye. But the more I studied the lines of his face and the way the shadows fell on it, the more focused I became.

"Shift your shoulders to the left a little bit. Actually, go ahead and shift your whole body to the left just a little." He smiled but kept his eyes closed as he did what I said. "Okay sit up straight and look at me." He did that too, and right when he opened his eyes, I snapped a picture. He smiled at my readiness, and when he did, I snapped another one. We had a little exchange of smiles as I snapped a few in a row.

It was my newfound attraction to his face that ultimately helped me take the photo we needed. So, in that way, it was a positive thing. That was the only good that could come of being attracted to Dominic, though. I knew it would break Laura's heart if I developed feelings for someone else so quickly, and I hated myself for it even being an issue.

I was thinking about that when Maria and Laura walked back into the apartment. We'd just finished, and Dominic had gone in his bedroom to return a phone call he missed while we were busy. I was unnerved by my own feelings and was relieved to see Laura so we could get out of there.

I thanked him again for everything on our way out. Laura asked him to email me a few of the best photos so she could look at them. I didn't object even though I dreaded having to stare at his face with Laura sitting right next to me, thinking my recent attraction to him might somehow be obvious to her.

She and I had lots to talk about when we left there. The Thanksgiving feast would take place in less than a week, and there was also the little fact that I'd somehow managed to make my way into the top ten photos of the contest.

I wondered what others had made the top ten, and exactly what place I'd come in, but I didn't ask either of those questions. Funny thing was, I think Dominic would have told me if I had asked.

"We have to RSVP to the Thanksgiving thing by Monday," I said later that evening when Laura and I were just hanging out in the living room. She was just starting to want to socialize with people again, and I wondered if a grand event like that might be too much. Truth was, I thought it might be too much for me and would like to be able to blame it on Laura. I wasn't so sure it was good for me to see

Dominic's palace when I was already having trouble dealing with his handsome face.

"I think we should go. I want to see Dominic's place. Don't you?"

"No. Not really. I mean, it sounds cool and all, but I'm good with just having a quiet Thanksgiving around here. I can't believe so many people show up to that thing if it's an hour away."

"Maria said it's worth going. She and Willy go every year. I think it'll be fun."

I couldn't believe those words were coming out of her mouth. "Fun?"

She shrugged. "Why not? Don't you like Dominic?"

"You mean as a boss?" I asked. I instantly began blushing guiltily. I stretched out on the couch and casually put my head on the pillow, seeming as nonchalant and unaffected as I could. She didn't answer me right away, but I just stayed quiet, lest I put my foot even further into my mouth.

"It seems like you two get along well," she said. "And there's nothing wrong with you finding love again, Rae baby. In fact, it would make me extremely happy to see you with someone like Dominic."

I felt a wave of about five different emotions wash over me at the same time.

1: Confusion about what I was hearing.

2: Disbelief that Laura would say something like that when I thought she'd view it as me cheating on Anthony's memory.

3: Fear that I could fall for Dominic and ultimately be rejected.

4: Elation at the thought of picking up the pieces and moving on with someone as wonderful as Dominic.

5: Hopeless at the thought that it could never really amount to anything. Seriously, he could have anybody he chose, and there were probably a hundred other girls in line ahead of me.

Not that I was in line.

I groaned at the ceiling since I didn't know what else to do.

"What's the matter?" she asked.

"Don't you think it's too soon to think about that?"

She came to sit on the ottoman in front of me and regarded me sweetly. "You're the only one who knows the answer to that question," she said. "*You* have to decide when you're ready, but I thought you should know that I have no expectations." She reached over and stroked my forehead before continuing. "I can't help but notice the way Dominic looks at you, and I want you to know I'm okay with it—happy about it, actually. It would make me happy to see you with him. He's probably the best match you could ever hope for."

I was tempted to smile when she said the part about noticing how he looks at me, but tried to hold it in. I absolutely couldn't believe she was giving me the go-ahead to like someone else. Before today, I'd never even considered it as an option, and here she was mentioning it as if she were reading my mind.

I stared at the ceiling and put my hand over my face as I spoke. "I was attracted to him today and I felt really bad about it." I didn't look at her but I could feel her reach down and rub my forearm as if to reassure me. My eyes filled with tears as I thought about Anthony. "It sort of feels like cheating," I said, trying not to let the tightening in my jaw affect my voice.

"You could be loyal to Tony's memory and still move on with your life, "she said. "He would *want* you to be happy. He would want you to be taken care of. I think Dominic could give you both of those things."

We were quiet for a long minute. "I don't think he'd go for me. Maybe for a fling or whatever, but nothing more."

Another minute passed with just the low murmur of the television in the background. "I'm not trying to encourage you to do anything you're not ready for, but Maria told me she thought he was smitten with you."

I put the other hand over my face, reinforcing my embarrassment.

"Did he email you the photos from today?" she asked.

"Yes," I said, not removing my hands.

"Can I see them?" she asked.

I grabbed my phone from its place on the ottoman next to her and opened the email he sent me earlier.

Rae,

Thanks again for the great photos. These haven't been edited, so please don't share with anyone besides Lu for now. I'll send you the final version once I finish editing it. You're more talented than you know, and I'm excited about watching you realize your potential. Let's do it again sometime, but with me behind the camera.

Best, Dominic

I scrolled past the message to get to the photos and handed her the phone. She gasped. "These are amazing Rae! Aww, he's handsome, isn't he?"

I smiled, thinking of the way I had gawked at him through the camera. "He's extremely handsome," I said, "...and smart, and rich, and all the other good things you can think of."

"Oh sweetheart, it makes my heart sing to think about you finding happiness with Dominic. I was so afraid I would hold you back by bringing you to New York with me."

"I can't even comprehend something working out with Dominic," I said, honestly. "He's just too good, and I've heard enough guys joking around at the deli

86

to know that these Italian men don't just run o
marry little blonde girls like me."

"My Anthony did."

"Yeah, but he was in Arizona. I think the guys
here get more pressure to date Italian girls."

"Where'd you hear that?"

"I heard one of the men that always sit outside
the deli mention the fact that I was blonde. He asked
what my maiden name was, and when I said
McBride, he said I must be pretty great if you and
Gianni were okay with Anthony marrying me. I
think he meant it as a compliment, but I got the idea
that I was a different breed to them."

"Don't listen to those old men," she said.
"Dominic is his own man and he can decide who he
wants to go out with."

I sat up and stared at her seriously.

"Do you honestly think he would ever go for
me?"

She reached out and cupped a hand on my cheek.
"Yes. And I think he already knows he would be
lucky to have you."

I put my head in my hands again, feeling
overwhelmed by the mix of fear and hope. "I can't
believe I'm even thinking about this," I said.

"I think you two could have something beautiful
together," she said. I was stunned speechless by her
support in the matter. I sat there for a few minutes,
not knowing what to say. I thought for sure she'd be

protective of Anthony and want me to wait years before I even considered moving on.

I reached out for my phone and she handed it to me. I glanced at the screen, taking in the photo. He was perhaps the most handsome man I've ever laid eyes on and I got butterflies in my stomach at the thought of having the green light to pursue him.

"I don't know what to do to make him notice me like that. I'm sure there are about a hundred other girls in line ahead of me, and I don't want to throw myself at him."

"Well, there's not much you can do with your work uniform, but we can get you all fixed up for the Thanksgiving feast and see if you can catch his eye."

I giggled. "Are you serious?"

She smiled down at me. "Why not?"

I spent the rest of the weekend thinking about Dominic and wondering how things would play out between us. It was the first time something else consumed my thoughts besides my sadness over losing Anthony, and it was refreshing.

Chapter 9

My photo of the one-man band was displayed with the others in the top ten when I got to work that Monday. It was surreal seeing a photograph I took displayed in an official setting like that. Because there were so few photos comparatively, Dominic had the final ten printed 11x17 instead of the original 8x10.

They were beautifully framed.

The presentation was amazing.

But the whole thing was still overshadowed by my developing feelings for Dominic. I can't explain how it's possible for me to love someone as much as I loved Anthony, and develop feelings for someone else just a few months after he passed away. I struggled with guilt about it, until for some unexplainable reason, it sunk in that Anthony would want me to move on and be happy. It sunk into my soul like an undeniable truth, and it wasn't just because Dominic was so appealing.

It seemed like once I came to terms with that, I couldn't get Dominic off my mind. I had no idea whether or not I had a chance with him for anything long-term, but I couldn't stop thinking about him. He consumed my thoughts more than making the top ten, and that was a miracle.

Thanksgiving week went by quickly. Laura stopped by the store twice that week. Once was to buy a pack of mints and vote for my photo (I didn't even see her that time). And the other was to meet me after work so we could go shopping for something for me to wear to Dominic's. Of course, she voted again while she was there.

It was the Wednesday before Thanksgiving, and shipping and receiving closed at 2PM. I was off work for the next four days, and felt giddy at the knowledge that within those days, I was going to try to make some sort of impression on Dominic.

Laura and I went to three different stores before my outfit came together. She also surprised me by making an appointment for me to get my hair done. The stylist cut my hair, put a shine treatment on it, and played up the waves by painstakingly adding polished curls with a curling wand.

Laura watched the whole process. I could see her reflection in the mirror and knew she was taking notes. One of the girls came over and put some makeup on me when Gwen, the stylist, was working on curling my hair. She stood between me and the mirror so I couldn't see what was going on until they were both finished.

I stared at myself slack-jawed. I usually just wore my hair pulled back, and seeing it cascading gloriously over my shoulders made me look like a different creature. Laura came over to see me up close when they were finished. She had her hand over her mouth, and was starting to tear up.

"If Dominic doesn't get on one knee and ask you to marry him, I'll eat my hat."

I gave her wide eyes for mentioning his name. As far as I knew, everyone knew what Dominic she was talking about.

"Seriously, I think I'm in love with her myself," the makeup girl said.

I gave her a big smile.

"I'm taking a picture of you for my Instagram," Gwen said.

"Me too," the makeup girl said.

They put me under a light and both snapped a few pictures. I was still in my work uniform and was relatively sure I looked like a big dork from the neck down, but it was hard not to beam when I loved what they did to me. Laura took a picture too.

"I'm sending this picture to Maria and telling her get ready for your new daughter-in-law," she said to me from the back of the cab on the way home.

"You are not!" I said, in a foreboding tone.

She laughed. "I'm just joking with you, but you look really beautiful, baby. I seriously want to email this picture to everyone I know so they can see you."

"Thanks for doing that for me. I never dreamed we'd get my hair done while we were out."

"I'm so glad it worked out," she said. "And I'm almost positive we could get close to reproducing this look tomorrow."

"I don't think I should go this far, do you?"

She gave me a confused look. "Why not? You look stunning. In fact, I thought about asking you to sleep like that so we could just keep it the same tomorrow and touch it up."

I cracked up laughing. "You're hilarious," I said.

"What? I think you should look just exactly like you look right now when you see him tomorrow night."

She and I met in the middle. We reproduced the look, only a slightly scaled back version. I almost felt like the boosted up version was false advertising. My outfit was dark, dressy jean leggings with a brown sweater that hung off one shoulder exposing a muted gold tank underneath. I dressed it up with necklaces, bracelets, and a scarf, and added some boots that complimented the whole look.

Laura wore burgundy. Both of us put a lot of effort into getting ready, and the ride to his house was exciting. Dominic's brother, Paul and William (one of the guys who helped us move into our apartment) were driving to Dominic's and offered to pick us up on their way.

Maria and Big Willy would be there too, but they spent the night before to help Dominic prepare for the party. The catering was hired out, but Maria was there to help Dominic manage everything. The feast was from 3 to 7PM with the meal being served in stages between music and other random entertainment.

In addition to his employees, Dominic had roughly twenty or thirty family members every year. Maria explained to Laura that ten or twenty of them usually ended up staying out at Dominic's for the night and crashed in one of his many spare rooms. Dominic loved hosting a big group for the night and always got in the kitchen with his dad and cooked a big breakfast the next morning.

Maria called Laura in the morning to make sure we were staying the night, and Laura thanked her for the invitation and told her we'd think about it. We thought about it for the span of a split second. In fact, the only reason she told her we'd think about it instead of agreeing right away was because she didn't want to seem to eager.

Paul and William picked us up at 1:30 in the afternoon, so we could get there when the festivities started at three. Paul was driving, and William offered to let Laura sit in the front. He made it obvious that he wouldn't mind being in the back seat with me, and Laura put the kibosh on that right away, saying she preferred the back.

The ride to Dominic's went quickly, and before we knew it, we were pulling up at his estate. There was a circular driveway with beautiful landscaping, and a valet waiting to park the car when we arrived.

Paul told him to park it in Dominic's garage, and he agreed easily before offering to help with our bags. Paul told him we had it under control, and he and William took not only their own bags, but also mine and Laura's.

"We'll put these in the back of the coat closet for now, and you can get them once you figure out where you're sleeping," Paul said.

We put our coats and bags away when we came in the door, and then walked through the entryway into the main living room. It was a huge, open space decorated with comfortable, eclectic furniture in rich colors. The foyer was elevated which gave us perspective on how packed it was. There were at least fifty people already there, and I got a good visual of most of them from where we were standing.

"There are a few other rooms opened up for the party," Paul said. "I'll take you around to them so you'll know where they are. If you snoop around at all, you'll come across a lot of locked doors."

"Oh, I'm not gonna snoop," I assured him. Laura was shaking her head adamantly, saying she wouldn't either.

He smiled. "Dominic opens the house once his employees leave. I was just telling you not to be surprised if you came across a locked door."

"You just tell us where to go, Pauly, and, we'll go there," Laura said holding her arm out for him.

He smiled and took it without hesitation. "We'll show you guys around and you can decide which room you like best. You don't have to stay in one place all night, but I will tell you it's best to be in the living room when the oysters come out."

I made a face like I didn't care for oysters, and everyone laughed.

"You finally made it!" we heard Maria squeal a few seconds later. We all turned to her, and one by one she squeezed us and wished us happy Thanksgiving. I was last in line for the hug just because of where I was standing, and she stopped to regard me after she gave me one of her famous squeezes. She stared at me for a few seconds before looking at Laura with wide eyes.

"She's the most precious thing I've ever seen."

I looked at Laura, feeling nervous and on the spot, and she smiled at me.

"She's a good one," she said simply.

"We were just about to take them around the house," Paul said.

"Have you seen Dominic?" Maria asked, ignoring his comment.

"We just walked in the door," Laura said. "This place is beautiful."

"Wait till you see the rec room," she said. "He's got jugglers in there."

As the day approached, my friends in receiving gave me more and more details about past parties. They told me he hired street acts to perform every year, so I knew to expect it. But being here and seeing it in person was different than I pictured— somehow more grand.

I hadn't seen Dominic since I took his picture. I'd thought about him non-stop since then and had built up the idea of him to unreasonable proportions. I was anxious to see if he could possibly be as good as I pictured. I was so anxious to see him that I almost didn't want to see him anymore.

"Dominic's gonna want to know you're here."

"What will I want to know?" I heard his voice say from the side of me.

I should have known it was coming because I saw Paul and William catch sight of something approaching.

"You'll want to know that Lu and Miss Rae made it," Maria said.

"Guess we're chopped liver," Paul said, being the first to reach out and hug his brother.

"Compared to the lovely ladies you came in with, you're pretty much chopped liver, bro," Dominic said, hugging him back.

"I tried to make Mrs. Milano sit in the front seat on the way over here so I could get to know Rae a little bit and welcome her to New York, but she wasn't having any part of that," William said, joking around.

"That's my girl," Dominic said, hugging Laura.

He came eye to eye with me for a few seconds before reaching in for the same casual greeting style hug he gave Laura. It was the eye contact before the hug that made my stomach turn flips. I could tell by the way he stared at me in those brief seconds that he felt some sort of attraction to me. His eyes roamed over my face with an expression that he was trying to restrain himself from saying something he shouldn't.

The hug was quick, and he regarded all of us as a group afterward. "I wish I wasn't in such a hurry, but I was just headed to talk to the girl in charge of catering,"

"I promised Lu and Rae I'd show them around anyway," Paul said.

William was standing next to me and, assuming Dominic was walking away, he stuck out an arm for me to take. I smiled gratefully and stuck my arm through his.

"Mom can show them around," Dominic said, glancing down at our linked arms with a scowl.

"We're going that way anyway," William said. "I wanna check out the jugglers."

"Actually, I need your help," Dominic said. "I think the girl with catering is gonna need a little man power."

"I'll show them around," Maria said.

"Thank you, Mom," Dominic said. He motioned for the boys to follow him as we walked off with his mom.

"I'm so glad you made it," Maria said.

"We wouldn't have missed it," Laura answered. "Rae's been hearing about this from all her friends at work. I can't believe this house. It's gorgeous."

"Dominic's sort of embarrassed about it. He's always been so humble and practical that it's hard for him to buy elaborate things like this." She smiled. "He'll tell you he got a good deal on it if you mention how beautiful it is."

"Did he?"

"He did actually—got a great price considering its size. Plus, we all begged him to do it. We told him it'd be the place we'd all come for family get-togethers."

"Did it turn out that way?"

"Definitely. We come out here for almost every holiday. He's got plenty of room, and we're all comfortable here."

Just as she said those words, we walked up to the open door that led to what I assumed was the rec room. There were twenty or so people spread out in small groups and I glanced around taking everything in.

There was a pair of jugglers who were getting set up in a corner of the room. They appeared to be talking to each other and warming up by tossing objects into the air and catching them. If they weren't twins, they were at least brothers—the similarities went beyond the matching outfits.

"Those are the jugglers," Maria said, noticing me notice them. "This room will be hopping in a minute once everyone arrives," she said. "It's really popular."

Chapter 10

The Thanksgiving feast was even more elaborate than I expected. It seemed like there was a surprise around every corner. There was a third, smaller room where the band set up. They played during the last two hours of the party, making that family room one of my favorite hideouts. It was loud and crowded in there, and I thoroughly enjoyed the music.

It was nearly seven o'clock, and I knew the party was almost finished, so I decided to ride out the rest of it while watching the band. Laura was talking with some of Dominic's family, so I'd been hanging out with Matt from receiving and his wife Angie.

"You better quit making sweet eyes at the lead singer," Angie said, whispering in my ear.

I smiled. "I'm not making sweet eyes. I like his voice, though. It's unique, don't you think?"

"I like it fine, but that's not what I was talking about," she said.

"What are you talking about?" I was only half-listening to her because it was loud, and there was a lot going on in the room.

"Don't look now, but someone's standing by the door watching you watch them, and he doesn't look like he's enjoying himself."

I didn't listen to her about not looking over there. I instantly glanced at the door when she said that.

My heart stopped. She was right. Dominic was standing there, and he wasn't even bothering to look around the room, his eyes were one hundred percent locked on me.

A flash of nervous jitters hit me at the sight of him. I smiled, and hoped it looked natural. He motioned for me to come over there, and I got up and headed toward him with no hesitation whatsoever.

"Are you in trouble," Angie asked. She was mostly joking, and I was relieved she didn't pick up on my feelings about him. I smiled back at them with fake fear and we all laughed as I began crossing the room.

"I forgot to ask if you and Laura were planning on spending the night. I should have mentioned it earlier, but I had a lot going on."

I laughed at the understatement. "Your mom made sure we knew we were welcome," I said.

"Are you staying?"

"I think so."

He gave me a satisfied smile. "Good."

We'd sort of made our way into the hallway as we spoke so we didn't have to yell over the music. Someone yelled his name from down the hall, and he looked up to see who it was.

It was a guy I didn't recognize who said, "You need to come talk to one of the valets. I think a set of keys might have gone missing." Dominic sighed and rolled his eyes before glancing at me.

"Go ahead," I said smiling. I gestured to the family room. "I'm gonna stay in here with Matt and Angie."

He looked slightly agitated, and I smiled internally thinking about Angie telling me not to make sweet eyes at the lead singer. I caught myself hoping that was the cause of Dominic's annoyance.

"I've got to go see to this," he said. "I just wanted to make sure you were staying."

"I think we're planning on it."

He headed toward the guy who was waiting at the end of the hall, and I went back into the room. I didn't try crossing over to Matt and Angie again since it was almost over.

That exchange took place at about 7PM, and the next few hours went by in an absolute blur. The guests who were spending the night stayed out of the way while Dominic, Willy, and Maria ushered everyone else out, and once the others were gone, we all came back out into the main room.

There were about fifteen of us spending the night, and we just sort of lounged around the main living area. Some of the faces were new, but I'd met most of them and liked them all. There wasn't a single person in the group that was hard to get along with, and I made easy conversation with everyone there.

Maria came to Laura and me to show us to the bedroom where we'd be staying. I didn't know what sleeping arrangements everyone else had, but I hoped they were as comfortable as ours. Laura and I had a small bedroom with a queen size bed and adjoining bathroom. I volunteered to sleep on a couch somewhere if someone needed the spot on the bed, but Maria assured us everyone had a place to sleep.

We all just sort of hung out together, being family, eating snacks, telling stories, watching TV, and teasing each other. It was like something you'd see in a movie where one side of the room busts out in an impromptu talent contest. That literally took place, and because I happened to be sitting on that side of the room at the time, I was forced to join.

I asked for a basketball, which took five minutes and a trip to the garage to obtain. Someone else sang a song while I was waiting, and by the time they got back, I was extremely nervous to have all eyes on me.

I had to trust my instinct. If there was one thing I knew how to do, it was spin a basketball on my finger. It was my one and only party trick, and by gosh, I was amazing at it. It was one of the only skills I ever learned from my grandpa. He was a ball spinning fool; he loved to spin basketballs on his fingertips and practiced constantly when I was a kid. I knew it was a weird skill for a granddad who was a makeshift dad to teach a girl, but it had come in handy a few times over the years.

My granddad didn't spin basketballs anymore. Now that the dementia was so bad, he couldn't –but that didn't stop me from bringing a ball to the nursing home before I left just in case.

Anyway, I spent a lot of my childhood having nothing better to do than spin balls with my granddad, and right at this moment I thanked God for that. Paul threw me the ball when he came in the room, and I caught it with a smile.

I stood and tossed it up a few times, testing the weight and feel of it. Laura had seen me do this routine, and she was grinning from ear to ear. She was grinning so profusely, I could hardly bear to look at her without laughing.

I tossed the ball into the air and landed it on my middle finger. It was already spinning when it landed because of the way I tossed it up, and as soon as I began using my other hand to swipe at it and increase momentum, the room went silent.

I heard at least one person hush the crowd as if they thought I needed to concentrate. I smiled and glanced at the group of people who were all focused on me. I pushed the spinning ball into the air, quickly hit it with my elbow, and then caught it again on my middle finger while it was still spinning.

At least five people made sounds of approval when I completed the maneuver, and I smiled at their cheers. I swiped at it a few more times to get it going again, and then repeated the process, this time hitting it twice with my elbow before catching it on my finger again.

More cheers.

Laura squealed with delight, and I smiled as I continued the act. It was a sequence I practiced nonstop as a kid, and had never lost the ability to pull it off when I needed it. I did three more tricks, each one increasing in difficulty.

Between the legs, off the head, and then for the grand finale, I bounced it off of several different body parts before catching it on my finger again. I caught the ball and tucked it under my arm as I took a bow.

Everyone yelled and clapped for me, and I plopped back onto the couch next to Laura feeling happy I had that trick up my sleeve.

William hopped into the spotlight, and after saying how hard it was to follow me, proceeded to do some crazy, double-jointed thing with his shoulder. That got a big reaction from everybody, and I was glad to fade into the background.

We stayed in there till about eleven when everybody dispersed, headed to their own quarters. Dominic and I stole glances at each other during the night, but neither of us could tell what the other one was thinking, and we never had time to be alone. I planned on trying to make an impression on him that evening, but the basketball spinning would have to do since we had absolutely no time alone.

He tried to talk to me several times, but someone always interrupted us needing his attention. It was 11PM when Laura and I settled into our room.

There'd been no time to try my charms on him, and once she and I had showered and settled into bed she said, "I know you didn't have much time to connect with Dominic tonight, but I really do think he likes you."

"What makes you say that?"

"I can just tell by the way he looks at you."

"I can't believe I got to spin a basketball in front of everyone." I said, laughing. "What are the chances of that?"

"With this family full of clowns, they're probably pretty good," she said.

We sat there and talked about the party for a good while. Neither of us could believe the trouble he'd gone to in order to entertain his employees, and the subject kept going back to Dominic and his generosity or how great he was.

Everyone mentioned eating a big breakfast the next morning, so I figured I had at least one more chance to let him in on how I was feeling before we left.

It was midnight, and we were just about to turn out the lights when Laura remembered she hadn't taken her meds for the night. She needed a glass of milk because if she took it with water, it was likely to give her a stomachache. I offered to go for her, but she insisted she wanted to do it. She put on a robe and slippers and tiptoed to the kitchen.

She looked at me with a wide-eyed, excited expression when she came back into the room a few minutes later.

I giggled quietly. "What?" I whispered.

"He's out there," she whispered back.

"Who?" I asked even though I knew good and well who she was talking about.

"He's sleeping out there on the couch, and he's alone!" she was so excited she could barely contain herself, and I just stared at her, feeling confused.

"Did you talk to him?" I asked.

She looked at me with the same confused look I was wearing. "I told you he was sleeping."

I shook my head. "I don't understand how that's exciting," I said. "There's really nothing I can do if he's already sleeping."

"Just go lay out there."

"What?" I must have had a comically confused expression on my face, because she laughed.

"Seriously, he's on the big sectional, and I think you should just go out there and lay on the other end of it. Take a blanket and pillow."

I studied her face as my smile faded. "You're actually serious about that?"

"Sure."

"Your plan is for me to go lay down by his feet?"

"Exactly."

"And what's supposed to happen?"

"All that needs to happen is for you two to get more than five minutes alone. Just go out there. He will tell you what to do."

I couldn't believe I was actually doing it, but one minute she was telling me to go out there, and the next, we were loading me up with a blanket and pillow. I tiptoed down the long hallway that led to the main living room. The sectional Dominic was sprawled out on was the largest couch in the room, but there were several others spread out, none of them occupied. I knew it'd be weird if anyone caught me doing this, and I trembled with nerves as I ever so quietly walked across the room.

He was sleeping soundly. I sat on the other side of the couch, debating whether or not I wanted to go through with it. I dreaded an awkward encounter with him when he found me lying at his feet, but had to trust that Laura knew what she was talking about.

I sat on the couch for a good five minutes before I gave in and finally curled up with my blanket and pillow. I had only been there for a few minutes, and I was extremely still, so it shocked me when Dominic turned and moved suddenly.

He sat up and glanced around at full alert. My eyes were open but I was completely still, half-hoping he didn't see me. I knew the whole point of me being out there was to be seen, but it was scary now that it was happening.

He squinted in my direction. It was dark in there, but not pitch black, and I could tell he was trying to make out the shadows. "Is someone down there?" he asked. He sat up straighter and leaned toward me to stare at the heap of blankets at his feet.

Never in my life had I been so speechless as I was right then, but I knew I needed to say something—unless my plan was to pretend to be asleep. *Was that even an option?* I quickly decided it wasn't.

"I'm here," I said softly.

He leaned even further toward me and extended his hands to feel around. He made contact with my ankle, and even though there was a layer of blanket between us, I loved feeling his hand on me.

"Is it Rae?"

"Yes."

"Come here."

"What?"

"Come over here so we can talk."

I stood up, and wrapping my blanket around my shoulders, went to the section of the couch where he was sitting.

Chapter 11

Dominic patted the space next to him, and I sat close enough where my body brushed against his. He didn't pull away from me. In fact, he turned and positioned himself where he could wrap an arm around my shoulders.

"What are you doing here, Rae?" he asked with a squeeze.

I wanted to say, "Laura sent me and she told me you'd tell me what to do," but I didn't.

I glanced up at him, and was about to say something else, but he continued, "Not just here on this couch, but what are you doing at my store? Why'd you come into my life?"

I leaned over and rested my head on his strong chest. I could feel his warmth against my cheek even though he had on a T-shirt. I felt so secure and comfortable that I never wanted to leave this position.

"I'm working at your store because Laura and I are working to pay off Frankie," I said, answering the only question I could.

He pulled back and looked down at me. "What do you owe Frankie?"

It took me a second to remember Dominic probably didn't know we owed him anything. "It was some debt from the dealership," I said, casually. "It's really not a big deal. It was less than we anticipated once we sold everything. I was just trying to answer that question about working for you. He's the one who got me the job."

We were quiet for the span of a few seconds. "What are you doing on this couch?"

Even though he was speaking softly, his low voice rumbled in his chest, and I just sat there quietly, enjoying the feeling of being next to him.

"I don't know how to answer that," I said in regards to his couch question. I *did* know why I was there but I was too shy at that moment to come out with it.

"I'm paying Frankie. Just tell me the amount and I'll write a check."

"That is not why I came out here," I insisted, pulling back to stare up at him.

He flashed me a gorgeous smile. "I hope not," he said.

"It's not," I insisted.

"I'm still paying Frankie."

"No you're not. I already owe you enough for everything you've done."

"Oh, you'll pay me back," he said.

His voice was serious and sincere when he said it, and I smiled a little, not knowing how to take that statement.

"Are we keeping track?" I asked. "Because I'm getting deeper in the hole with you every month if that's the case."

"I'm definitely keeping track."

"How am I supposed to pay you back?"

He thought about his answer, and by the time he spoke, I thought he might ignore the question and change the subject. "Marry me," he said.

I giggled and leaned into his chest shyly. He pushed me back by the shoulders and stared right at my face from a few inches away. It was dark, but not dark enough that I couldn't see the seriousness in his expression.

"Rae, are you here right now because you want to be with me?"

I considered denying it, but nodded slightly.

He stared at the ceiling and let out a sigh, and then he caught me up against his chest, squeezing me tightly to him. "Thank God! I knew you were Tony's and I didn't want to do anything to disrespect his memory or hurt Lu, but I've wanted you from the very moment I saw you, Rae. I feel like maybe you and I were meant to be together. Do you feel like it too?"

Tears of relief and joy had already begun streaming down my face, so instead of answering out loud, I just nodded.

"Do you think Lu would be okay with—"

I nodded again, and he put his arms around my head and shoulders, holding me closely to his chest again.

He let out a long sigh.

He held me like that for what must have been five minutes. I couldn't think of any words, and it seemed he couldn't either.

"I guess I should go back to the bedroom," I finally said, even though it was about the last thing I wanted to do.

He breathed another long sigh. "It's probably best since we have so many people in the house," he said. "I'm sure Lu's missing you, and I don't want anybody else to get the wrong idea." He hesitated and squeezed me again. "You know what? I can't bear to let you go. Just lay beside me for the night. Let's get some rest. Dad will be up first. He'll be out here for coffee at seven on the dot, but as long as we get you outta here before then, nobody will see you."

"I can't just lay next to you," I said, even though I really wanted to.

"If someone comes out during the night, they'll assume…"

"I know we can't be seen together like this until we let everyone know what's going on, but I can't stand to let you go back in there. What if you sleep at the other end of the couch like you were before I woke up," he said. "We can set an alarm and get you out of here before Willy wakes up, but at least I'll know right where you are while we get a few hours sleep."

He'd just said a lot of words, but the part about letting everyone know what was going on was what stuck with me most. *What was going on exactly?*

112

Was he serious when he said he wanted to marry me?

We'd just been sitting here holding onto each other, and the longer we did, the more I started to doubt our situation. I thought he might have just told me that I should sleep by his feet because he couldn't bear for me to leave. My stomach did a delighted flip at the thought.

"Did you say you wanted me to lie down over there?" I asked, pointing to the spot by his feet.

"I *want* you to lie down beside me, but since that won't do, I'll have to settle for having you down there. Just make sure you share my blanket so I can feel your feet."

I sat up like I was about to make my way over there, but he stopped me. He brought his lips to my cheek and put a gentle kiss on it. My insides were buzzing with butterflies, and I drew in a shaky breath while his lips were still resting on my face. He left his mouth right there by my ear when he whispered, "I thought I was going to be able to stop at your cheek, but I can't resist your mouth, Rae. The temptation's too great."

"I'm glad," I whispered breathlessly.

He stared at me for a few seconds before letting his lips touch mine. My gut ached in an almost crippling bout of butterflies. The contact was brief and he pulled back a few inches to stare at me afterward.

"You need to go lie down there before..." He cleared his throat. "We'll make this official come sunrise."

So I stayed at Dominic's feet till the morning.

I woke to the feel of him shaking my shoulder. I opened my eyes to find that he was on his knees next to the couch, leaning over me. I smiled instantly and he smiled back. "I've been sitting here staring at you for five minutes. I was so entranced I almost forgot to wake you up."

I sat up. "Is your dad up?"

"Not yet. He'll be out here in a few."

I gathered my blanket.

"You can get a couple more hours sleep if you want," he said. "Most of them won't make their way out here till nine or so for breakfast."

I yawned. A little more sleep sounded good, but I was so excited about Dominic that I didn't know if I'd be able to rest.

"Are you going back to sleep?" I asked.

He smiled and cupped a hand around my face. "No. Dad says he tries to be quiet if someone's sleeping out here, but he doesn't. He'll want me to get up and drink coffee with him so he can tell me about all he saw at the party." He stood up. "How much?"

"What?"

"For Frankie. I don't want you to go back to Laura empty handed. I'm sending you in there with a check. How much?"

"You're not doing that," I insisted.

"I want to. How much?"

His tone was so matter of fact that I just told him the amount without even thinking about it. "It's right at twenty-two thousand."

"That's it?"

I laughed.

"I thought when you said it was from the dealership we'd be talkin' at least a hundred."

I laughed again and rolled my eyes at him even though he couldn't see me because he was walking toward the kitchen. He stood at the bar for a minute, writing what I assumed was the check.

I was standing with my blanket and pillow in my hand when he returned. He had an athletic build and looked handsome walking toward me even in his pajamas. He handed me the check and then took me into his arms without giving me the chance to look at it.

"You have no idea how happy I am that you're mine," he said.

"I can't believe this is happening," I said.

"Do you want it to happen?"

"Yes."

"Me too."

I looked up at him, and popped up to place a little kiss right on his mouth. He smiled broadly and squeezed me by the waist. "I can't get enough of you Rae McBride."

"Well, you have to or else Big Willy's gonna catch us out here."

He gave me a last squeeze and a kiss on the cheek before letting me go. I ran silently into the bedroom, feeling like I might just explode from happiness.

I didn't look at the check until I got into the room. Laura appeared to be sleeping when I opened the door, but she stirred at the first sound I made. I glanced down at the check, which was made out for $25,000.00, and I smiled as I made my way to the bed to sit next to her.

I didn't show her the check right away.

"What happened?"

"It seems that Dominic and I might try to give things a go," I said. I couldn't bring myself to say he was going to marry me. It seemed too unreal.

"What did he say?"

Then suddenly, I couldn't stand it anymore. I had to say the words. "I think he might have said he wanted to marry me," I said, my voice sounding uncertain.

"What'd he say?" she asked, wide-eyed.

I thought back to our conversation and tried to remember exactly how it went but couldn't.

"He found me right after I went out there," I said, starting at the beginning. "He seemed startled at first, but invited me to sit next to him. We talked and he held me there for a while. That's when he told me he wanted to marry me, I think."

"Well, what did he say?"

"He said he was paying the debt to Frankie and when I asked how I'd ever repay him, he said marry me."

"Just like that?"

"Just like that," I said, dazedly. "I can't believe it myself, actually. It can't be true, can it?"

She reached across the bed and grabbed my hands. "Of course it can," she said. "I knew it by the way he looked at you!"

"Do you think he feels obligated?" I asked, hoping she'd say I was being silly.

She reached up and put a hand on my chin, regarding me sweetly. "Who in their right mind would be obligated to be with you, Rae? He's as blessed to have you as you are to have him. More maybe."

I smiled and held up the check I'd forgotten about for a minute. "He said he didn't want me to come back to you empty handed."

She took the check from me and stared down at it. "This is too much. He can't be doing this anyway, but this is too much."

"I didn't even see what it was written for till I came in the room."

She put the check down and drew me into her arms. "I can't believe this is happening," she said. "I didn't think I'd ever understand happiness again, but you've become my daughter through all this, and my heart feels truly happy with this match, Rae.

Dominic is going to take as good of care of you as Tony would have." She wiped at her eyes.

"I'll never forget Anthony," I said.

"I know you won't, and I know Dominic respects his memory."

"That was another thing he said—that he liked me before, but didn't want to act on it because he thought it might hurt you or me for Anthony's sake."

"I knew he was feeling like that," she said. "Maria even mentioned it. That's why I told you to go to him."

I sighed. "I don't want you to go out there announcing our wedding plans in the morning," I said. "Let Dominic mention it first just in case I'm wrong."

"You're not wrong. He loves you I can see it." She held up the check. "I can see it with a bunch of zeros right here. People don't just walk around handing out money."

"That could have been for you. You know, since you're family."

She smiled sweetly at me. "He loves you."

I smiled back. "I don't know what to say besides thank you. I don't know where I'd be right now if it wasn't for you."

"Rae, you have no clue what you've done for me. You've given me life where there was none."

I hugged her. "Dominic mentioned getting some more sleep, but I'm not sure if I could. He said Big Willy will have breakfast around nine."

"That's a couple of hours away," she said. "We'll be lazy for a bit and then get you pretty to go out there."

"I'm not expecting him to make an announcement or anything," I warned.

"I know he won't rest till everything is settled," she said.

We sprawled out on the bed and talked for a while about possibilities before deciding to get dressed. I was so glad we'd gone shopping the day before because I had a really cute hoodie to sport when I went out there. It was white with stripes across the chest in various muted colors that made it look old school. I loved how it fit me, and was happy to have something that made me feel confident. I wore the same jeans I had on at the party, but slipped on my pink converse instead of the boots I had on the night before.

Laura helped me put my blonde waves into a messy braid that hung over my right shoulder. I took my time with my makeup, but was careful not to overdo it. By the time I was ready to go out there, I felt happy and anxious to find out what was around the next corner.

Chapter 12

Laura and I walked down the hallway at 8:30AM to the sounds of a kitchen full of people. We could hear talking, and we slowed as we approached the living room. She stuck her arm in front of me to make sure I didn't continue walking.

"I heard your name," she whispered.

"She ain't Italian, I'll tell you that," someone said.

"Do mom and dad care that she's not Italian?"

"Of course we don't," a woman's voice said. I assumed it was Maria.

"Willy might mind, did you ask him?" a guy said.

"I'm going out there," Laura whispered at that, but I stopped her.

"Dad doesn't mind," I heard Dominic say. I smiled knowing it was him. "I told him my plans right when he woke up this morning. He couldn't be happier for us."

"And your plans are to marry her?"

"Yes."

"You barely know her, what if she's an axe murderer—a non-Italian axe murderer."

"That's it, I'm going out there," Laura said.

I put a hand out to stop her again. "Whoever it is, he's just playing around," I said. "I can hear it in his voice."

"I know, but I still don't want him saying things like that."

"It's fine," I whispered.

"I can't say I blame you for questioning my sanity on this," I heard Dominic say, "but I can assure you it's something I've thought about since I met her. It's the best decision of my life—the only choice I had."

I heard a female in the room let out an *awww,* at his sentiment.

"She's a good woman," a man's voice said. "Just look at how she treats Lu."

"I'm going out there," Laura whispered, unable to handle it anymore. "I'll tell everyone you'll be right out."

"There she is right now," I heard someone yell a few seconds later when Laura showed her face.

"Morning everyone," she said. Several people spoke at the same time, and it was difficult to discern any one conversation after that.

"Where is she?" someone said loudly enough for me to hear.

"She'll be out in a second," Laura said.

Again, there were multiple low conversations and I couldn't hear any of them clearly. I took a few deep breaths before working up the nerve to walk out there. I peeked around the corner shyly as I walked into the main room.

Dominic, who was on the other side of the room talking to Laura, caught sight of me. He smiled before turning to tell Laura something; and seconds later, he was crossing the living room, walking in my direction at a good clip.

He seemed genuinely relieved to see me, and as he got closer and continued picking up speed, I realized he wasn't going to stop until he ran straight into me. He took me into his arms with such force that I giggled.

"I told everyone our plans," he said.

I glanced up at him. "What'd you tell them?"

"That I'm marrying you."

"You did?" I whispered so no one else could hear.

He turned me by the shoulders to face the group of family and close friends who were staring at us curiously.

"I think everybody here wishes Tony were still with us," he said to the group at large. He hugged me to his chest, but I craned my neck to stare up at him when he spoke. "I know it's been a hard time for Aunt Lu and Rae, and I'm happy that it worked out where I could step in for Tony."

I couldn't stop the tears from rising to my eyes, and I turned in his arms to bury my head in his chest. His big hand stroked my hair gently, and I tried to hold back the tears.

"Aunt Lu, you're the only one I haven't talked to about this. Rae said you two had talked about it."

I turned just enough to glance at Laura who was nodding and wiping at her eyes.

"You know I'm gonna take care of her, right?"

She nodded again as tears poured down her cheeks and she continued to wipe at them.

"It's settled, then," Dominic said. "Purely out of love for my dear cousin, and having nothing to do with the fact that she's kind, talented, and so very beautiful, I'm going to marry this girl at the soonest possible opportunity. If any of you have a problem with it, please see my dad who will kindly spit in your eggs."

Everyone laughed, including Dominic, whose chest shook. "Seriously, I want you to know that I couldn't be happier, and I want you all here to celebrate when we're married."

The whole group clapped and came over to embrace us and give their congratulations.

"I'm so glad we were here to see this!"

"I know you two are going to have a beautiful life together."

"Thank you for bringing her to us!"

So many kind words were being said that I felt overwhelmed with happiness, gratefulness, and love.

"She can't be in the contest if she's your wife, it wouldn't be fair," someone said.

I looked up to see a guy named Vince who was one of Dominic's cousins but also worked on the floor at Nic's. He'd entered the contest himself and knew my photo was one of the finalists.

Dominic looked down at me with a shrug. "Yeah, you're not in the contest anymore, sorry."

I stuck my lip out, but in a silly way that showed I didn't care all that much. "The contest ends in a few days," I said. "I doubt we'll be married by then."

"Yeah, but you don't even work there anymore, right?"

I scrunched up my face like he was confusing me, and he gave me a squeeze. "We'll talk about all that stuff later," he said. "But you're not in the contest anymore. Vince is right, I'd definitely cheat for you."

"See?" Vince said.

"Did you cheat already?" I said with wide eyes.

Vince gasped like he hadn't considered that. Dominic put his hands up in surrender. "I promise I did not. You can ask Debbie and Bill. They had access to the totals all month."

He was looking at me when he said it, but the explanation must have satisfied Vince because he didn't say anything else. Everyone took a turn at congratulating us before we all went back to hanging out and eating breakfast. Laura and Maria went right to work talking about wedding possibilities while Willy made eggs to order.

***

I married the stunningly handsome Dominic Russo four months later on a beautiful Sunday afternoon. The wedding was late March, and we assumed it'd be cold, but it turned out to be a gorgeous spring day, which was a welcome surprise. We got married in front of a hundred guests in the same church where most of the family said their vows for generations before us.

We thought about having everyone over to the big house for the reception, but they would have all spent the night, and we knew we'd want privacy after the festivities were over. We had the reception at a place Maria loved for it's old-world Italian décor. It was in the city, but when you entered, you felt like you were being transported to another time and place.

There was food, music, and dancing for two hours after the wedding. We danced a traditional dance called the Tarantella where everyone held hands and danced in one direction before switching back. The process continued as the music sped up, and by the end of the song, we were all dizzy and laughing.

Anthony and I hadn't performed any Italian traditions at our wedding, so it was my first experience with the dance. The same was true for the last tradition we did before we left the reception headed for the apartment.

"Ladies and Gentlemen," Big Willy said, getting everyone's attention. "We're gonna honor Nic's Italian heritage by performing this sacred wedding tradition. With the breaking of this vase, we pay tribute to their future together. As they break it, we'll think of all of the beautiful gifts each of them bring to this relationship, and the limitless potential that lays in front of them as a couple. I want everyone to think special thoughts and focus all your love and best wishes up here on this couple."

Willy handed Dominic the vase, and he tossed it at our feet, causing it to break to pieces. We both stepped on the pieces, causing them to break into a zillion tiny shards. Everyone cheered.

"As you all know," Willy said, "The number of pieces signifies the number of happy years Dominic and Rae will have together. They've done a thorough job of smashing that vase, so the future looks bright."

Everyone laughed and gave us a round of applause, and within ten minutes we were in the backseat of the car headed for our apartment. Dominic and I saw each other a good bit at the reception, and had danced together a few times, but everyone wanted our attention, and by the end of it all, I found myself thirsty for the sight of him.

My head was spinning with the thrill of it all. My ears were ringing from the music, and I had a permanent smile on my face. The trunk was full of gifts, and the driver and doorman helped us get them on a cart to bring them upstairs.

"Do you want to open a few of these?" I asked, as I took them off of the cart.

"You can open all of them if you want," he said, "They're yours."

"They're yours too," I said.

"You're mine. That's all I care about."

I flashed him a smile that I felt from the top of my head to the tips of my toes. "How about I open three of them and save the rest?"

I opened a dish, a clock, a mixer and a few gift cards before making my way to Frankie and Viv's box. There was a card attached to it with a gift card to Crate and Barrel, which I stashed with the others I'd already opened.

I opened the box to find what looked to be an old shoe. I glanced up at Dominic with a confused expression, and he shrugged.

"It looks like a shoe," I said.

He smiled. "I see that."

"There's just one of them," I continued.

"Yep."

"And it's used."

"Yep."

"Do you think it's Frankie's?"

"It looks like something Frankie would wear."

He reached into the box and removed the worn out leather dress shoe before looking inside of it. He fished a piece of paper from the toe and unfolded it.

"What's this about?" I asked.

He shrugged as if he had no clue whatsoever, and then read the note out loud.

Dominic,

Vivian told me I owed you this. I'm not sure what it means. She said it's something her great uncle told her about—like a receipt for paying the debt Gianni owed. She couldn't really explain the whole thing, but she's a sucker for traditions, and was adamant that I send you this. It was the shoe I was wearing when Lu handed me the check, which Viv said is significant. I told her it was lucky for her it wasn't my snakeskins, or I wouldn't have sent it, tradition or not. It's probably not significant to you, but here's my shoe nonetheless. We want you two to know how excited we are about the match with you and Rae.

With love and best wishes,

Frankie and Viv.

"I love how weird you Italians are," I said, smiling up at him.

"That's not an Italian tradition," he said. "I've handed out lots of checks in my life and never once had someone take off their shoe and hand it to me as a receipt."

I shrugged and smiled. "At least it wasn't his snakeskins."

He laughed and then stared at me smiling. "I'm sorry for what it took to get you here," he said. "But I'm so happy you made it."

I looked at him, trying to put into words what was in my heart. "Everything that's happened in my life, tragic or happy, led me to this moment. I've never been happier than I am right now, Dominic, and I'm thankful for each and every event that led me to this point." I stared into his dark eyes wondering how I ended up with such a man. He was sweet, and smart, and loyal, and my love for him had multiplied ten times during the past months.

Dominic and I didn't know each other the way a husband and wife know each other during our courtship. We talked about saving it for the night of the wedding, and even though it was extremely difficult at times, we made it.

It had come down to this, and I knew tonight would be the night we'd both enjoy what we'd been craving. I was nervous and hoped I could please him the way he deserved. The thought of trying sent a wave of desire through me, which was reflected in the way I stared longingly up at him.

"If you keep looking at me like that, we're not going to be able to open any more of these presents."

"Why's that?" I asked innocently, biting my lip.

"Because I'll be too busy carting you off to the bedroom."

"Being carted off might not be so bad," I said with a casual shrug. And with that, he scooped me into his arms and carried me down the hall.

Epilogue

It had been just over a year since Dominic and I got married, and I woke up every day thankful for my life. It was hard to believe that I'd been so low at one point. I thought about Anthony and knew in my soul that he'd be happy with the way things turned out.

Dominic took care of both Laura and me with no questions asked. I moved in with him when we got married. Laura thought about moving in with us since we had plenty of room in his big house, but she knew I'd be staying in the city at the apartment quite a bit, and she didn't want to follow me back and forth. She said she'd miss the city anyway and felt comfortable in her apartment with so much family nearby.

Dominic and I split our time between houses, spending a few days in one place and then going to the other. I liked the change of pace, and took pleasure at being able to experience both. I still got to see Laura about three times a week when I stayed in the city. Our frequent visits were the reason she felt at peace with staying at her apartment.

Of course, it was hers now. Dominic bought it from Frankie not long after we got married, and we gave it to Laura as a Christmas gift. Frankie didn't want to sell it at first, but Dominic talked him into it.

Laura took great pride in it and had been fixing it up with the help of Little Mike and a few others.

She'd gotten back in the swing of socializing with friends, and made an effort to get together with Maria, Viv, and the others on a regular basis. We had settled into a routine that was like a dream come true. I got to see Laura on a regular basis while having privacy to start a family with Dominic.

And start a family was exactly what we did.

Nearly two months ago, I gave birth to our first son. We named him Luke. We were as in love with him as we were with each other, which basically meant it was a big love-fest everyday at our house.

He was only seven weeks old now, and Dominic and I had each taken thousands of photos of him. We both loved photography, and taking photos of Luke just gave us an excuse to stare at him. One thing's for sure, this kid was being well documented.

I spent a two full weeks at the big house after I had him, but had been back in the routine of splitting our time between there and the apartment lately. Luke came with me wherever I went. He was an easy-going baby who'd been a joy since the day he was born. Laura got her hands on him anytime she could, and when we stayed in the city, she'd often come to our apartment to hang out and help me care for him.

Sometimes while she was there, I'd walk around with my camera for an hour or so, and when I'd come back home, it was like I hadn't seen him in a year. It was still the same way with Dominic. When we were in the city, he spent a good amount of time at the store, and my stomach still turned flips every time he returned home.

Dominic was at the store this morning, and Luke and I had plans to meet Laura and a few of the ladies for lunch. Laura and Maria saw him on a regular basis, of course, but there would be other ladies in the group who'd be meeting him for the first time.

I got us both dressed and the driver took us to Laura's. I thought about having him take us all to the restaurant where we'd be meeting the others, but it was a nice day, and the restaurant was only a few blocks from Laura's, so we walked.

I had a beautiful, elaborately expensive stroller that had been part of a package of gifts from the employees at Nic's. I hadn't brought him by there to meet everyone yet, but had plans to do it soon. Lunch with the ladies would do for today.

We went upstairs at Laura's for a few minutes before heading to the restaurant. It wasn't uncommon for me to bring prints of photos for her to inspect. I did it just about every time I saw her, to the point where she almost expected it.

I handed her three 5x7's of photos we'd taken in the last few days. She always liked to scrutinize them and try to decide if Dominic had taken it or if I had. It was one of her favorite games, and she was usually right about it even though we had similar styles.

"We're bringing these to the restaurant for the others to look at," she said. "In fact, I'm bringing some of these other ones."

She crossed to the little catchall where she stashed the photos I brought her, and grabbed most or all of them. We headed out and walked the four blocks to the small pub Maria suggested. I'd been there before and liked it, so I was glad to hear that's where we were going. Maria text to let us know she'd be bringing Paul's new girlfriend with her and for us to do recon when we could since she didn't know a thing about her yet.

Viv came as well, and when we got to the restaurant, Viv, Maria, and the new girl named Allie were already sitting down waiting for us.

"We ordered appetizers," Maria said, when we walked up. "Hey baby, you look amazing," she quickly added, reaching out to hug me. "Hey Lu, you're not so bad yourself," she said, squeezing Lu as well. "And where's my beautiful little grandson." She said it in a cooing baby tone because, even as she spoke, she was leaning over his stroller to get a look at him. She pushed back the canopy and gasped. "I think you've grown and it's only been three days," she said. She reached in and took him from the seat carefully before sitting at the table with him cradled in her arms.

Viv came to stand over her shoulder so she could get a good look at him. Allie peered at him but

133

didn't' get up. She wore an easy smile that gave me a good first impression of her.

Maria introduced her to Laura and me, as we got settled at the table.

"I brought some pictures," Laura said, handing the stack of about fifty prints to Viv.

"I'm not sure if I've seen all those, so you'll have to pass them over here when you're done," Maria said.

Viv nodded at her, but then looked at me with a stunned expression. "These are gorgeous, Rae! I can't believe how beautiful they are." She flipped to the next one and stared at it. "I can't believe you and Dominic took these. They could be in a photography book."

I said, "Thank you."

But it was overshadowed by Laura saying, "I keep telling her that. She could put out a coffee table book with all these pictures."

"She sure could," Viv said.

"I'd buy it," Maria said.

I giggled. "You guys would buy it because little Luke's the star."

"Yes he is," Maria said, staring down at him. She looked up at Laura. "Lu, we got ourselves a good one here," she said.

Laura nodded. "I know it. He's a fine specimen."

"His mama too," Maria added, smiling sweetly at me. "She's been better to you than seven sons."

"You're not kidding, Laura said with tears in her eyes. "She's my angel, and I thank God for her every day."

"You girls are gonna have to stop this," Viv said, wiping at her eyes. "I have to go back to work and nothing on my face is waterproof."

We laughed as all the ladies simultaneously touched the corners of their eyes with napkins.

"Oh, look who it is," Viv said, smiling as she looked over my shoulder. I turned to find my knight in shining armor walking toward me with a huge smile on his face.

"I couldn't let you have lunch right down the street and not come by," he said. I stood to hug him, feeling relieved by his presence even though I'd seen him only a few hours before.

He placed a kiss on my cheek and held me at his side as he greeted everyone else at the table. The appetizers came at that moment, and Maria insisted he stay and have lunch.

"I can't," he said, regretfully. "I have to take a conference call. I just wanted to come by and see my lady and my number one boy."

His mom turned so Dominic could get a good look at our bundle of love.

"Those photos are amazing, Dominic," Viv said.

Allie agreed saying she'd never seen such creative baby pictures and we should open a studio. Dominic gave Allie some good-natured warnings about his brother, which made us all laugh.

135

I'd been standing beside him, and he gave me a little squeeze. "I'll be home around four," he said.

I stared up at him. "I can't wait."

He leaned in and put a kiss right on my mouth even though we were standing in the middle of a restaurant.

"I love you," he said.

I was so smitten that I reached up and touched his cheek.

"I love you too."

He smiled and gave me one quick kiss before waving to the others and making his way out of the restaurant.

Dominic and I were as happy together as two people could be. We knew beyond the shadow of a doubt that we were supposed to be together, and that knowledge brought a sense of security and contentment to our relationship that we were both thankful for every day.

We often joked about the fact that were destined to be together, saying it was so undeniable that someone from our lineage would probably end up saving the world.

The End

But Ruth replied, "Don't ask me to leave you and turn back. Wherever you go, I will go; wherever you live, I will live. Your people will be my people, and your God will be my God. Wherever you die, I will die, and there I will be buried. May the Lord punish me severely if I allow anything but death to separate us!" When Naomi saw that Ruth was determined to go with her, she said nothing more.   Ruth 1:16-18

God has not promised skies always blue,
Flower strewn pathways all our lives through.
God has not promised sun without rain,
Joy without sorrow, peace without pain.
But God has promised strength for the day,
Rest for the laborer, light on the way.
Grace for the trial, help from above,
Undying sympathy, unfailing love.
-Anonymous

Thanks to my amazing team, Chris, Jan and Glenda... you're the best!